CRYPTIC

PUZZLES, BOOK ONE

JODI PAYNE
BA TORTUGA

Cryptic
Copyright © 2021 by Jodi Payne & BA Tortuga

Edited by LC Hinson

Cover illustration by AJ Corza
http://www.seeingstatic.com/
Cover content is for illustrative purposes only and any person depicted on the cover is a model.

ISBN: 978-1-951011-56-7

Electronic edition published by Tygerseye Publishing, LLC, July 2021
Printed in the USA

As always, to our wives.

1

_____

"Jesus, Crash. What the hell was that?"

It was a rhetorical question, so Derek shook his head at the patrolwoman and got into his car. *That*, was a woman in her late sixties who'd been strangled to death. It wasn't something anyone ever wanted to see, and he wasn't surprised that Leslie was still putting it together in her head. He was too.

Leslie had offered to drive, but he was glad he hadn't let her; the steering wheel gave him something to do besides crack his knuckles and wring his goddamn fingers. She put on her seatbelt as he pulled away from the curb, and he rolled his eyes. Sure, it was the law, and maybe he hadn't earned the nickname "Crash" for his pristine driving record, but it was only eight blocks to the precinct. What could possibly happen?

Leslie looked over at him. "You've got to be tired of this."

He could feel her eyes on his face but didn't look away from the road. "Tired isn't the right word." Angry. Worried. Baffled. Stressed. Nervous. Sleepless. Lots of words came to mind. Tired didn't begin to cover it. This was murder number three in as many months, and he was livid. The problem was he had no idea what he was going to do about it yet. He had to do something, obviously. As the detective assigned to all three cases, everyone was looking to him for answers.

But he didn't have any. Not one.

He wasn't going to admit that because he wanted to keep his job long enough at least to get his one-year performance review. Plus, he was pretty sure half the precinct already thought he was an idiot, so he kept his cards close to his chest and hoped to hell someone on his team would find him something he could sink his teeth into this time.

Something other than "this one was strangled too". That was just terrifying. Three people, all strangled, but with nothing else in common? That was a nightmare. A serial killer shaped nightmare.

His nightmare.

His phone buzzed, and he resisted the urge—manfully, he thought—not to roll down the window and toss the fucking thing out into the street.

His mind was racing, dealing with images of the swollen, black tongue and missing wedding ring of his latest vic and the inevitable horror that came with knowing he had to tell the family. He didn't have the time or the capacity to deal with distracting emails or calls on his phone.

Especially while he was driving. Leslie might have kittens.

"You'll call—"

"I'll contact the family. I'm on it. You want me to be there again?"

"Please." Hell, yes. He had to be the bearer of bad news, he accepted that, but Leslie would cover the awkward things like hugs and Kleenex. Somehow she always managed to find words, good things to say. Better things than, "I'm so sorry," which was all he ever seemed to be able to muster.

He was sorry, though. Genuinely. He was drowning in regret that he hadn't found the asshole responsible for the first murder, let alone the second, and now there was a third. He had no intention of giving bad news to a fourth family.

He pulled into the garage and parked in his reserved spot. "You'll—"

"I'll text you when they've arrived." Leslie never let him finish a sentence. Just as well, he didn't much feel like talking. He needed to think.

His phone buzzed in his pocket as they got on the elevator, reminding him he had messages waiting. Who the hell emailed anymore? His team would have texted. His friends texted. Oh. Maybe it was his Verizon bill.

When he clicked the button, though, it was a familiar name.

Matthew Herrera.

Asshole.

The son of a bitch had worked a couple of high-profile cases ten years ago, had a breakdown, and had disappeared into the desert. Until now. Now the bastard was crawling up his dick like a Brazilian fish.

Back when Herrera was relevant, Crash might have had more interest in whatever the profiler had to say. But ten years later, after radio silence, after the country had forgotten Herrera even existed, he just skimmed the emails, humoring the guy and pretending to have patience like he did with Mrs. Rosen down the hall when she told him about everyone that came and went in the building while he was gone all day.

He'd nod and smile, say thank you, and disappear into his apartment before his takeout Chinese got cold.

This time he didn't even skim. He hit delete. He had more important things to do than to give time to a desert-dwelling, nosy hobbyist. The asshole was crazy, and when he found out which joker in the department gave out his email, he was going to hit someone.

Hell, maybe he'd just start socking pricks in the mouth until someone confessed.

Good idea, idiot. Maybe one of them will knock some sense into you.

"I'll text you in a bit, detective. Get some coffee. You look like shit."

Derek blinked at Leslie, only just realizing they'd stepped off the elevator. Wow. "I'm fine. Thanks, Leslie."

Fine. Just another body to deal with. No big deal, right?

Coffee was the right answer though, or part of it, and he got himself a cup and took it back to his office. Then he pulled a pack of Camels from his top drawer, flipped open the lid and inhaled, deep. The tangy scent of the tobacco was just enough to make his hands stop shaking but not enough to make him not want to smoke.

Dammit.

He tossed the pack back in the drawer and shut it tight.

His email beeped again, Herrera's name popping up.

Delete.

Fucker.

He was going to have to block the bastard.

He could solve this mess on his own. He and his team would figure this out. He sure as shit didn't need some has-been playing armchair quarterback. Right?

Right.

Maybe.

He glared at his phone as the familiar voice of doubt rattled him, made his fingers itch.

Maybe you can do this. Or maybe you'll fuck it up in spectacular fashion.

He told that voice to shut up and was rewarded with a *you're a hack and you know it* headache.

Oh, fuck it.

He reached for his phone. He'd just read this last one. One more just to prove to that bitch of a voice that he didn't need the help of a lunatic recluse.

He took her wedding ring, didn't he? Did he choke her with Gene Harris's tie? The text shocked the shit out of him. Who was feeding this fuck information? *and STOP IGNORING ME!*

What the actual fuck? The names of the victims were given to the press after he'd notified the family but the details—like the wedding rings—were not. His thumbs hovered over the screen for a millisecond as he debated whether to respond.

When I find out who is leaking shit to you, I'm going to have their ass arrested. And yours. You know, I might just have your harassing ass arrested on principle. Go the fuck away.

He hit send without thinking about it. He did a lot of shit without thinking about it, impulsivity was his greatest weakness, and also his greatest strength. Some people called him stupid, some people called him brave. That was cool; he'd understood from a young age that they were the same thing.

He was so over this New Mexican hermit, but that doubting voice told him to text the ME next, so, also impulsively, he did.

Angie, was there a wedding ring in Mrs. Cohen's throat? Was it Gene Harris' ring?

Before Angie answered, his phone beeped, the New

Mexico number popping up again. *I'd love to see you try, detective. I'm helping.*

Motherfucker.

He got three-quarters through with a scathing answer when Angie answered him. *Ring yes. How the fuck would I know whose it is? Man's. Big.*

He stared at Angie's text, then sent her a thank you, followed by kissy lips and a middle finger.

The simplest answer was usually correct. But what was the simplest answer? Herrera had hacked something? Herrera was in on it? Herrera had made a lucky guess?

He tapped Herrera's last text and dialed the number, waiting for the asshole to pick up. Helping, his ass.

"Menos mal." Deep and growly, obviously pissed—Herrera had a voice meant to be listened to. "I've been waiting for your call."

Waiting for...for fuck's sake. It was like he'd been summoned. Arrogant prick. Derek didn't bother trying to keep the frustration out of his voice. "What do you want, Mr. Herrera?"

"I assumed it was what you wanted, no? To find this asshole."

"I want to know where you're getting your information so I can plug the leak, and then I want you to stop contacting me."

"Fine. I'll speak to Detective O'Reilly. I assumed as you were trying so desperately to fill Martin's shoes, you might be willing to listen."

"Desperately—who the hell do you think you are?" Oh, this guy was lucky New Mexico was a longer reach than his arm. "There's nothing to listen to. You've been driving me batshit with your lunatic emails."

But...

"I'm not fucking desperate."

But Herrera knew about the ring.

He took a deep breath, swallowed his pride and lowered his voice. "The ME found the ring, but we don't know who it belongs to yet. Tell me how you know about it."

"Because I pay attention. Case number 259313. Vivica Reyes. Found dead from manual strangulation with Andy Lipinski's ring in her throat."

259313... 259313...

Derek pulled out a pen and scribbled the number on his palm.

259313 Reyes Lipinski

"I'll look into it." That case was forever ago, and wasn't the killer still in prison? "Are we done?"

"Until you find a young woman dead in a laundromat strangled with one of Mrs. Cohen's scarves. Absolutely." A dark chuckle sounded. "Good evening, detective."

There was no way Herrera could know that. The scarf was an educated guess he could have made if he thought about it and the laundromat? A total fabrication meant to try to impress him. It was a load of insane bullshit.

He noted, however, that neither of them had hung up the phone.

Bottom line, he didn't want to find another dead body at all. Anywhere. Woman, scarf, in the laundromat, in the billiard room with the candlestick, whatever. Right or wrong, he didn't give a shit. He couldn't afford to. It just needed it to not happen again.

"How long do we have?"

"Six days, if he stays to type. It'll be close. Six block radius. Did you find any threats at the other scenes?"

Fuck, he wasn't going to sleep at all. "Nothing obvious, but we're still sifting through things. Some personal items and their cell phones are missing. Six days. Six days? Are you sure?"

"Cell phones... All smart phones?" He heard mad typing, faster than he could think, for fuck's sake.

"Yes. None of them have been powered up since they disappeared; we've been watching them."

Six fucking days. Six days and he hadn't even been able to put together an MO yet. He needed to get the team together.

"So he's younger, I'll bet. He's found a younger one..."

"He who? What? Younger than who?"

"If I knew that, Rick Adonai's fucking partner would be in jail, don't you think?" Oh, that hit a nerve, didn't it?

Adonai had a partner? He didn't recall reading there was anyone still on the loose. "Partner? I thought that case was closed. No one ever talked about a partner."

"I thought so too, until Denise Lewis. Note I've been emailing since then."

Denise was the first. A young nurse, newlywed, nothing tying her to the other two but the missing cell phone.

"Noted. But your emails are long and rambling, and I couldn't manage to retain anything. I gave up reading them. You come off like a lunatic. You know that, right? If you had something direct to say, why didn't you just say it?"

I think Adonai had a partner. How hard would that have been?

The laughter that rang out was shocking. "I said what I meant."

"Well, I found it esoteric and disorganized. I couldn't follow it at all. You do much better in conversation." The emails were insane. Long and rambling, circling around a point—if there was a point at all.

"Things have become infinitely clearer over the last few days. Infinitely."

"Yeah, well. I'm out of infinite. If you're right, I've got six days."

He had a strong team and top forensic experts on the job, but they were almost nowhere on this. If Herrera was right, he was going to have to ask for help. He was going to have to get into the killer's head. The accomplice's head. One more murder, and his next step would have to be the FBI and then he'd really look like an idiot. He would prefer to see this case solved in-house.

At this point, even a lunatic's help was preferable to none. "When can you get out here? What time is it there? Can you get on a flight tonight?"

"That's not an option. Sorry."

He blinked. *What?* "I'm sorry? Not an option?" Surely there was a late flight out, but...right. He was working with a nut job. Oh. Maybe it was money. "So...first thing in the morning, then? It's on my dime."

"No. You do your job there. I—don't travel well."

Oh. That wasn't going to work. People here were already looking for reasons to discount him, and he wasn't making it very difficult on them. The last thing he needed was to say he had a source in New-Fucking-Mexico that was profiling for him. *He's brilliant, but he's lost it, and he won't get on an airplane so...*

Nope.

"Listen, Herrera—Matthew. Or Matty. Can I call you Matty? Listen, Matty. You need to appreciate something, okay? I'm the newest detective on the block. And the youngest. And I'm—" He sighed. He was fucking desperate, wasn't he? "I have questions. I have to understand how you know what you know. I have to see the profile. If you're telling me we really only have six days..."

"I'll send you a profile. You'll have it tonight. Goodbye, detective."

Click. Well, okay then.

Crash stared at his phone and shook his head as the dust settled. What the hell was he doing? This was no way to go about an investigation. He needed something concrete. A real starting point. Not some disjointed babble. He needed to get off the bus to crazy town.

He picked up his phone and texted Angie again.

Tell me you have something.

The knock at his door interrupted him, and Leslie poked her head in. "They're here."

"Thank you. I'll be—no, I'm coming."

No answer from Angie. Okay. He had a job to do. God, he hated this part.

He took a deep breath and followed Leslie.

2

"Fuck, Ben-baby. How is he fucking doing it?" Matthew stared at the ME reports from six years ago. Rick Adonai's victims. All nine of them. They were spread across four computer screens, the light drowning out the full moon over the Sandias.

He'd been called in after the fourth vic.

Penelope Little. Pretty little blonde nursing student from Alabama left in a laundromat. He'd packed a bag, kissed his partner goodbye, flown to New York into a nightmare. One that had never ended.

"You need to breathe, Einstein."

"You know I hate that." But it made him smile. Still. "I want to know who his partner is."

He'd thought it was true, back then. Now he knew. He also knew that no one had any reason to believe him.

They would, once the next two victims were found.

A nurse in a laundromat.

A gym enthusiast on a roof.

"Wouldn't that be easier to figure out in New York? That's where he is..." Damn Ben. And damn being practical.

He shook his head, his belly going tight with a flood of pure terror. He was safe here, comfortable. This huge adobe fortress was their—*prison*—safe space. "No. No, everything they need, they can get here. You're here."

"You need to work. You'll feel better. You're happy when you're working."

"I am working." Matt dropped his head to his hands. "I'm happiest with you, love. I can't go. You know I can't."

"Get busy then. That nurse is counting on you, Einstein."

"Right. I'll get the baby detective a clear profile. If he's smart, he'll save her."

Not that he'd saved anyone. Not until the end.

Smart might not be enough.

His phone vibrated next to his keyboard with a new text from the detective. Detective Derek Wheeler. Crash Wheeler. Matthew had done a lot of research, to the extent that some courts would classify as stalking.

Born in Metuchen, New Jersey. Thirty-one, ex-marine, ex-smoker, gay—which consequently made him the ex-son of his Catholic parents.

I'm pulling the file on Adonai's case. Send me anything you have that wouldn't be in it.

A simple "please" would be nice, wouldn't it? But Matthew wouldn't get one. Not while the detective was focused. Right now it was all about getting the job done.

Stubborn and insecure—common traits to find together. Had a little money put away that would cover a good stretch of rainy days. Lived in a modest apartment. Shopping records showed the he liked Nikes, a dive bar downtown, and killed a lot of goldfish. Hardworking, good-looking, and single.

"Do you like him?" Ben was like a mosquito in his ear.

"I don't like anyone. I don't even like me. He's harmless." Harmless and scared that he couldn't do the job. Still Bob Martin said Wheeler was a good man, so Matthew would give him a chance. "I just want him to get Adonai's partner."

"Don't you mean Rick's partner?" Ben whispered, voice suddenly so close.

"Don't you ever say his name!" He saw the rictus of his face in the monitors as he screamed, and Ben was gone.

His phone woke up again, though.

Wait. Even if he has an accomplice, how is Adonai operating from prison?

Don't you have his correspondence? He's got to be talking to someone. He didn't have access to that. Yet.

I don't have shit on him. I only knew to ask for his file ten minutes ago.

Matthew rolled his eyes. *Haven't you read any of my emails?*

He left off the 'dickhead', but it was absolutely implied.

Did I not just tell you they ramble and are unreadable nonsense?

He heard the "asshole" in the reply, so the detective was obviously reading him well.

It made him grin, to be honest. He appreciated a person with sense.

Unreadable? Bah. You just aren't following along.

Fine. Just get me the profile ASAP, Einstein. You wanted in, you're now in.

He sat back, blinking. Oh, Ben was so fired. *I'm on it. Name's Dr. Matthew Herrera.*

Einstein had a PhD too. Not at seventeen, though. You win, Matty.

I'm an overachiever. Sue me. He'd been blessed to have a professor as a mother and a surgeon as a father, both of whom had his back, as far as academics went.

He had been tall for his age when he went to his auntie's in Houston, and he'd fit in with the other grad students, fucking and drinking and smoking weed, but he was a lightweight, and addiction ran on both sides.

Rehab had sucked, except for Ben.

Ben had been magic, through and through.

Counting on you. Talk soon.

Matthew read the text again. It seemed strangely sincere for someone whose last flurry of texts were so stressed and sarcastic.

He shook his head, standing to go refill his coffee cup and—

Marissa's face popped up on his phone. *Boss?*

What?

I brought you a sub. It's on the counter. Eat. It.

I will. Thanks.

You want me to come up? I'll type your profile for you.

He winced. Mari was supposed to be on a hot date tonight. *Did you chop him into little pieces and feed him to that cat?*

I haven't found him. Yet. Pls Boss. I'll bring ice cream.

Come on up.

Sometimes he needed a little company, and he hadn't seen her in over a week. Her apartment was on the first floor, and he stayed on the third. The kitchen and media room were on the second, and were largely unused.

Mari could have let herself in but didn't, knocking instead barely a minute later. She was wearing oversized sweats, her hair was up in a messy bun, and her eyes looked a little on the puffy side.

She had a couple of pints of ice cream in her hands and held them out. "Cookie dough and mint chocolate chip."

He took them both, set them aside, and hugged her tight. "Men suck."

She hugged him back, nodding against his chest. "Total assholes. Tell me you have work for me to do."

"We're sending a profile to a detective in New York. He's not a big reader. I need you to clarify me."

Mari laughed and let him go. "Ah. He's not a big reader, and you're not the most succinct. Not a good combination. You eat your sub. I'll translate. Let me put these in the freezer."

Work cheered her right up. He could relate; it was all about keeping the brain busy.

"I don't know what I'll do when you decide to leave me." He'd had Mari as assistant for five years, and she was invaluable to him—she knew when to tell him no, when to holler. Hell, she'd even threatened him with a shoe once.

"I do. You'll crawl back into the endless research loop you were in when I was stalking you for a job. Fortunately for you, I have no plans to go anywhere yet. Also, you're the only one that gets it so..." Mari kept the pint of cookie dough and dug through a drawer for a spoon.

"Good. You're important." The call of the information on the screens was too important to ignore, so he went back, comparing ME reports for the second victims, with that missing phone in the back of his head.

Mari reached around him and shut off his monitor. "Oh, look! A sub! How did that get there?" She put it on his keyboard and opened a laptop on a nearby table.

"Evil bitch. Oh. Oh, Dion's. Green chile veg?" She was so good to him.

"Greek dressing. Fruit cup. Eat, you old queen."

Matthew laughed, and the act felt rusty, unused.

Mari chuckled along with him, then eyeballed him every so often while he ate, reading something on her laptop screen. "Wait. Oh my God. Adonai is back? Matthew, why didn't you show me this stuff sooner? Are you okay? No wonder you look like shit."

"He had a partner. I thought so then. I know now." He stood up and started pacing. "I was just...you know. It was a bad case."

"I know, I...know." Mari watched him, then took a breath. "Okay. So the answer is to nail this guy this time. Let me catch up." She looked back at her screen. "What are you thinking? They must be in touch, right? Why now?"

"I don't know. It's been six years, four months, give or take. But I need the prison correspondence. He's got to be talking to the partner."

"Did the detective hire you? Is he going to send you what you need?"

"I think so? He offered to fly me out there..."

Mari glanced over sharply, her look incredulous. "You're going to New York?"

"Are you serious? There's nothing I can't do from here." Ben was here. She was here. His world was here.

"Oh good." Mari went back to reading. "Tell me what you know about the accomplice."

"He's following the type, the clues. He's not leaving crosswords this time, but he's taking smartphones."

"Copycat?"

"It's possible, but Adonai's talking to him." And he didn't believe this was happening again.

"Smartphones. Huh." Mari started scrolling and clicking and searching on the laptop. "Have any of them turned back on?"

"Don't know. Just found out that bit tonight. I need the detective to be more forthcoming." He had a woman in the ME's office, but they wouldn't know about the phones, dammit. "There's got to be something about them."

They'd never found any souvenirs at Adonai's apartment, but at that part of the investigation he'd...been elsewhere.

"I'll make a list of things we need from the detective. Well, why would a killer take a cell phone? Because there is something on it he doesn't want us to find, right? They're lousy souvenirs; they're password protected, and the service will be turned off..."

"Yes. So social media? He meets them on Facebook? Twitter? Snapchat? Adonai doesn't have access to those, or he shouldn't." His screens were still off, and so he grabbed a pen and started scribbling.

"Those are very public too. And not...intellectual enough. You know what I mean? Adonai likes to show off how smart he is." Mari looked at him—or, more like through him, which she did a lot when she was thinking.

"Okay. Intellectual... Political boards? There's a hundred thousand places for the bastard to hide." He picked his phone up, searching through his apps. He researched on Twitter sometimes, but... "Dammit. I need Adonai's letters!"

"It's on my list." Mari waved a hand at him. "Hey, Matthew. Sit down and eat. I have the profile you were working on for the detective, so let me get that cleaned up, okay? He's not going to give you anything until he sees this." She took a big bite of ice cream.

"Right. I just... I want to know, you know? I want that fucker shut down." It was vital.

"Me too. And I would bet this detective...uh, Wheeler, is totally invested too. We're all focused, right? But what did you tell me? Cross your T's. Sit. Eat." Mari started typing like a madwoman, fingers flying on the keyboard.

"Right. Sit. Eat. It's all good." Then he needed to apologize to Ben, say his mea culpas so he could focus.

3

T his was bullshit.

All of it. Everything. It was fucking bullshit.

Records had brought him a stack of boxes—one for each of Rick Adonai's victims, plus a couple full of notes and files left by his predecessor. Eleven boxes in all. Derek stared at them, heart pounding, sick to his stomach.

He wasn't cut out for this. He was supposed to be a marine, flying jets and following orders. Point, aim, shoot, and get the fuck out of there. Simple and straightforward.

His stint as a patrolman had been a fine second career, and right now he wished to God he'd stayed there. He could have put in his twenty-five and retired to run a touristy fishing business out of Long Island or something. He'd taken the detective test because people'd said he should; they said that was what a guy did, that was how he moved up in the chain of command. He never for one second believed he'd pass it. He was supposed to fail and validate what he already knew about himself; that he was just a hardworking dumbass making ends meet.

Ambition wasn't in his DNA. He didn't even have a

college degree. And now look where he was. Three murders, no doubt a fourth one on the way, and somehow it was his job to figure this shit out and stop it.

Him.

Crash Wheeler, a dipshit with more concussions than he had brains. He might as well have been trying to stop a semi barreling down the highway with a brick propped on the gas pedal.

Fucking bullshit.

He glanced at his phone, noting the new email that just came in from Herrera. He sighed and paced his office, working through his choices. He could ignore Herrera and keep on the investigation with his team, or he could hitch his wagon to a seemingly credible and slightly insane profiler who wouldn't get on an airplane to come help in person.

Who was he kidding? This shit was on him. At this point he'd take help from Mickey Mouse.

He needed Herrera.

"Okay," he said out loud. "Procedure. Call the team in, get them reading. Get everything to the profiler. Work the problem." It would be a lot easier if the fucking profiler were here in New York.

There was a knock at his door and Leslie appeared with a box in her hands. "From the Supermax prison in Colorado."

Case in point. Evidence was here, but profiler was in fucking New Mexico.

"Put it on my desk and go call the rest of the team in, please? Tell them to bring toothbrushes. We're not leaving until we know what our next move is."

"Will do. You know what we're looking for?"

The temptation to snap back, "a serial killer," was huge.

Vast.

Fucking gigantic.

"I was contacted by Matthew Herrera, the profiler on the Rick Adonai murders a few years back. He believes Adonai had an accomplice and may be in touch with him again. These are the files on those victims. I need all of you to read and summarize them and get us all up to speed on that case."

He was going to bite the bullet and read through the stack of incoherent, rambling, brain dump emails from Herrera.

"This is turning into a really big case, Leslie. Really fucking big. And if Herrera is right, we only have six days to stop the next murder."

"Herrera? Like Dr. Herrera? The dude from New Mexico? He's a fucking lunatic, you know that, right?"

He glared as Jack Evers came in and propped himself on the desk.

"What the fuck do you mean?"

"I mean Adonai killed the son of a bitch's gay lover. That's how Herrera found him. The bastard found Adonai's apartment here, and there was a crossword waiting for him."

"Jesus Christ." Derek shook his head. Adonai had made it personal. That explained why Herrera didn't want to fly out here. "I'm not sure it matters whether he's a lunatic if he's right. And he's the only lead we have right now."

But if Herrera was wrong, they'd both look like lunatics.

"The latest victim had a wedding ring in her throat. He called and told me she would. He was right."

"I'm not saying he's not brilliant. I'm saying he's insane. Rumor is he locked himself in that house in the desert, never comes out. He's obsessed with Adonai." Jack shrugged. "What if he's feeding the accomplice-slash-copycat information?"

"Herrera?" Anything was possible but... "Assuming he's angry that Adonai killed his lover, why would he do that?"

"Hello! Crazy!" Jack rolled his eyes. "Who knows why a crazy guy does anything?"

He couldn't rule out the idea, but he wasn't really feeling it either. He picked up a box and handed it to Jack. "Summarize that for me before midnight, then come get another one."

"Oh, man, tell me you're buying the pizza." Jack was an ass, but the man loved his job and, given enough food, would work like a dog.

"Pizza tonight and bagels in the morning are on me. It's going to be a long night. What do you think, Leslie?"

"I don't know, Crash. It's possible I guess. But I don't think you go that kind of crazy after losing a lover. I think he'd be more likely to go after Adonai in prison or something than I would to copycat."

He nodded. "We'll leave everything on the table for now. Grab a box and call the others." He went back to his desk and opened the box from the Supermax, then pulled out the last handful of letters and took pictures of them, firing them off one by one in texts to Herrera.

There's a big box. Too many to send. These are the most recent. This would be easier with you here. Reconsider.

It took about five minutes for a response to come in. *I need them all. I can't work like this.*

Arrogant prick. Derek wanted the help, but this my way or the highway bullshit wasn't working for him. And he wasn't sending evidence to someone his team thought was legitimately suspicious no matter what his gut told him.

He needed to have the conversation about Herrera's

lover in person to clear the guy. He maybe could find a reason to arrest Herrera but that would make things even more awkward than they already were.

I could have it all scanned for you, but that will take time we don't have. Pack your suitcase.

When there was no answer, Derek frowned. He'd expected push back, not silence.

Come on, man. I need you here.

He didn't have much patience on a good day, and this was not a good day. He called Herrera and listened to the phone ring.

"What?" Oh, looked like he wasn't the only one on the grumpy side of the fence.

"I can have my people check flights and get you on one." Derek was absolutely not holding his breath. Not.

"I—"

A woman's voice sounded. "You can't, boss!"

"Who is that? You absolutely can. I'll uh... I'll compromise with you. You pick the hotel, and you tell me what you need."

Jack stared at him. "Is that him?"

He nodded.

"Pick the hotel? He's not a celebrity."

Derek waved Jack off.

"Get me one close to you with good Wi-Fi. You pick me up. I know what you look like. I don't leave the hotel room."

Shit, Herrera was coming.

"Boss!" The woman's voice shouted again.

Herrera shouted back. "I need to see the correspondence, Mari! I can't work without data!"

"It's a deal. Who is that? Matty. Matty, listen to me. You want to stop this guy? You need to come." *Like, now. Tonight.*

"Find me a flight. If you're not at the airport, I'm turning around and coming home. Are we clear, detective?" The tension in Herrera's voice was raw and obvious.

Okay. Yes. Good.

"I'll be there. I'll take care of the hotel. Are you coming alone?"

"Of course. Text the details."

He heard the voice of the woman arguing as the line went dead.

"He's coming." He'd make all the arrangements himself and be at the airport early. He wasn't taking chances.

Jack laughed. "Herrera's actually gonna show?"

"Get to work. I want to be caught up before he lands."

4

Matthew grabbed his carry-on and his rolling office, kept his eyes open, and looked for Wheeler—he'd seen more than one picture of the man, and he had no intention of staying here for one second longer than he had to. He'd already had enough of lights and noise, people. He'd upgraded to first and bought the seat next to him, just so he didn't have to have anyone breathing on him, touching him.

He could handle this. He could.

A day looking at the letters, then he could go home.

One day.

All he had to do was find a blond cop who needed help.

Wheeler turned out to be easy to find. The detective was waiting for him right on the other side of security and raised a hand to get his attention. Blue jeans, T-shirt, black leather jacket that stretched across wide shoulders.

The guy came toward him holding a tray with two coffees in one hand, and offered the other. "Derek Wheeler."

"Mucho gusto. Dr. Herrera. Thank you for picking me

up, no?" He shook Wheeler's hand, his belly going twisted at the touch.

"No problem. Do you have any other luggage? I have a car waiting to take us to your hotel." Wheeler started walking. "And coffee."

"Coffee. I have everything I need here." Computer, tablet, phone, Xanax, Reds, warm socks.

"All right. Let's go then." The detective led him through baggage claim and out onto the sidewalk. Wheeler held up a hand, and a black car pulled up. "Driver's name is Kit, and he works with the department often. I trust him."

He nodded, but he knew better. Trust was pointless. He trusted Ben and Mari. That was it.

Wheeler opened the back passenger door as Kit climbed out of the car and opened the trunk.

"Let me help you with your luggage, sir."

He handed over his knapsack with clothes, and kept his computer and files with him. Those didn't leave his sight.

"I got you the best room I could find," Wheeler told him as he got in the car. "You said close, right? I mean, there are nicer hotels, but they're a subway or a cab ride away. This one is three blocks. It's small and kind of no-frills, but it's clean, and the owners are friendly. There's a diner on the block and a decent bar, with a little grocery on the corner."

Wheeler handed him a coffee from the tray the guy had been carrying all this time. The detective's concern for his comfort seemed genuine despite everything the man must have going on. "I thought you might want to drop your stuff off, and then we could talk over breakfast?"

Jesus. Breakfast? It was still not even his bedtime yet. He slept in the heat of the day, really. Mostly. When he slept. He wasn't a sleeper. "Bueno."

"Bueno. Cool." Wheeler nodded and took a big sip of

coffee and then rubbed his eyes with the heel of one hand and sighed. "I'll have someone on my team bring the box of Adonai's correspondence over to you. What else do you need?"

"I want to know if he is doing crossword puzzles, and if he is, what he's doing with them." Adonai had worked making the fucking things—that was how he could torture the victims. He made the fucking clues that, filled out just right, would scare the living fuck out of people.

"I sifted through the letters a couple of hours ago, and I didn't see any crosswords. Not a one. I actually thought that was odd."

"Nothing?" That made Matthew's teeth itch. How the fuck could there be nothing? "Well that's all bad, isn't it? Fuck me."

He grabbed his phone and started typing notes.

"No xword found in corr. New cipher? Word search?"

"I don't know, is it? That's what you're here for, Einstein. I'm just a grunt with a gun waiting to go after the guy." Wheeler sipped his coffee and looked out the window. "You're right. It's all bad. Really bad. I have to figure this out —we have to. I can't...four is too many."

"No shit." He would figure this. He had to. Today. He needed to go home.

The rest of the drive was quiet, both of them stuck in their heads. Finally, the car stopped in the middle of a quiet block, and Wheeler got out. "This is it."

The hotel had an unassuming look, just a green awning stretching from the sidewalk, up a flight of stairs to a set of double doors. The lobby was clearly a hotel lobby, though, with tons of marble and chrome, and the reception desk at one end of the room was tall and official looking.

"You want me to...the room is in my name so I'll just...

yeah." Wheeler left him standing there and went to check-in.

Cute.

Maybe more than cute, not that he noticed. But he wasn't dead. Not yet. He had work to do.

He waited, making notes on his phone about ciphers and puzzles, keeping one eye on Wheeler.

"Eighth floor." Wheeler came back shuffling his wallet and the card keys from one hand to another until he got it all sorted out and handed him one. "Your key. I'll keep the other. Elevator is that way." Wheeler pointed with the hand holding the wallet and then stuffed it in a back pocket.

He grabbed his rolling office and followed. Eighth floor huh? The eighth floor was lucky in China. That mother had murdered her family on the eighth floor in Galveston—less lucky in Texas, obviously.

In the elevator, Wheeler tapped the extra room key against the back of one hand like it was a pack of cigarettes. "So who was the woman shouting at you on the phone yesterday?"

"My assistant." Mari wasn't anyone to the detective and didn't need to be. She was safe from Adonai. A nonentity.

"Like a personal assistant? Or a research assistant?"

"Both. She's my assistant, full stop." She made his world work—from groceries to mail to research.

Wheeler squinted at him as they got off the elevator. "Okay, man. No need to get defensive. I didn't ask if you were sleeping with her or anything."

"You don't have to. You know I'm queer as a three-dollar bill. She's not on my lovemap." And he preferred masculine types, when it came right down to it.

"Room 803." Wheeler pointed. "Put your shit down, and let's go get some food. I have questions."

He let one eyebrow lift, and he stared, more than willing to wait the officer out. He wasn't the perp here; he was here to help, and he deserved basic manners, whether or not the man was interested in offering it.

"803," Wheeler repeated, staring back at him. "What?" It took longer than it should have for the guy to get it, but the detective finally sighed and rolled his eyes. "Really? Put your shit down, *please*?"

Better. "No problem. Come on in."

He opened the door, fascinated for a second by the light trails coming off his fingers.

Wheeler followed him inside and looked around. "I asked for a street view at least so you get some light...looks like you got it. Cool."

"It works. Thank you." He put his bag on the bed and stowed his laptop bag. Soon he could get to work. First there would be the questions, the mini-interrogation wherein Wheeler decided whether he was brilliant, insane, or both.

"Ready to eat?" Wheeler headed for the door, which had barely been closed a minute. "We can try that diner down the block."

"Works for me." If they had coffee, he'd be fine. "Lead the way."

Wheeler cared too damn much for his job, but that was to be expected. The detective was so new he squeaked, and was...looking to make a difference? Move up in the department? Make Mommy and Daddy love him again? So many sparkly possibilities.

It was a bright morning, and the shadows were long, leaving half the street gleaming and the other side dark. The diner wasn't more than half a block walk, and they definitely had coffee. The server put a silver pot of it down in the middle of the table.

"What can I get you?" She asked, looking bored and tired. She must have been finishing her shift.

"Two eggs over easy, bacon, and wheat toast for me." Wheeler was looking at his phone, thumb scrolling, and didn't even look up to order.

"Just toast for me, please." He did look up, nodded to her. Someone had hit her, not long ago, the bruise almost hidden by the makeup.

She looked back at him, and sighed. "White, whole wheat, rye, pumpernickel, gluten free, English muffin..."

"Pumpernickel." The temptation to ask for chicharrons con chile was huge, but this woman was tired, her feet hurt, and someone liked to beat on her, so maybe not.

She turned around without a word and stuck their order in a pass-through window. Wheeler reached for the coffee and poured for them both. "Okay. So, I've been over all the vics. The first three from this guy are a lot like the first three of Rick Adonai's vics, right? So that's why you think a woman in a laundromat?"

"No, I was reading tarot cards, and it came to me in a dream. Jesus was there, along with his unicorns." He saw patterns; that was his world. It wasn't magic. It was just how his brain worked. "Possibly a nurse or a nursing student, but I'm not sure about that. He'll have to find one that works. Just scrubs might be enough."

Wheeler looked back down and silently stared into his coffee mug, tracing the porcelain lip with his thumb. Eventually, the guy sighed and shook his head. "Okay. I hear you. Maybe I am an idiot, but I'm the idiot assigned to this case. I was up all night with the case files on Adonai's victims, and I went back and read all of your emails too. It's a lot of information for one long fucking night, and I'm doing the best I can here, okay? No one else is going to die on my watch, damnit. I think a real idiot doesn't know when to ask for help. I'm asking. I need you."

"I'm here. We need to know how he picks. We know how Adonai did it. He loved the game, the torture. That's why I posited that he had a partner. The manner of killing is straightforward, relatively fast."

"I just texted my team, so the box with the correspondence is being delivered to your hotel room. It'll be there after breakfast. He's not fucking with me or my team like he did with Detective Martin. He hasn't left puzzles or anything. He hasn't tried to contact us."

"The partner just wants to kill, but there has to be a reason he's started up again, a trigger. It'll be in those letters. It has to be." The bastard—big fingers, latex gloves, no other forensic evidence, not even a fucking hair—wasn't going to be quiet for years and then decide one day to recreate his greatest hits for fun.

"Why would he take their phones and leave the bodies? It's not like we're trying to track them. And he never turns them back on so he's not trying to lead us to him or...anywhere."

"What's different about phones now? They had smart phones, iPhone 4 was the new one, so we're not talking flip phone era..." What did the guy do with them? Protect them? Hoard them? Watch... Could he open the phones? Nothing Matthew saw suggested a high level of intelligence or tech interest, but he could be wrong. What if he was watching them, watching their lives after they were gone?

"I don't know. Better cameras? Instagram?" Wheeler looked at the phone in his fingers again. "Snapchat?"

He made some notes on his phone. "Could be. He has to find them somehow. Choose them. What are the chances Adonai has access to a phone?"

"Impossible. He's at USP Florence. There's a reason they call it the Alcatraz of the Rockies, you know? He doesn't have access to the outside world. His incoming mail is screened and censored, he gets one fifteen-minute call a month, and he's never used it."

"Okay." Impossible? He shook his head. The phones meant something.

"But does Adonai need access? Maybe the phones mean something to the accomplice. Maybe they're just a souvenir...maybe he plans to turn them on eventually?" Wheeler glanced up at him, the look uncertain. "Maybe he just doesn't want us to have them."

"Maybe." That was as reasonable as any of the other eighty-thousand reasons they could come up with. The correspondence would help. He hoped.

Their food arrived, and the waitress set it down and then started pulling condiments out of a pocket in her apron— ketchup, tabasco, a handful of jellies in little plastic containers, more creamers for their coffee. "You guys still good on coffee?"

Derek picked it up and nodded, then refilled both mugs while it was in his hand. "Yeah. Thanks."

Coffee got a thank you. Huh.

"So how did you get into this business? I mean, other than being a genius. Did you go to school for it?"

"My masters is in linguistics, and my PhD is in Human Factors, the interactions of people and other elements of a system. Patterns are my specialty. So in effect, yes. I did." Everything had a pattern, whether you intended it to or not.

"So you're a few degrees ahead of me..." Wheeler laughed but it sounded uncomfortable. "I earned my pistol expert marksman badge in the Marines three times though, so you point me, and I'll shoot."

"Thank you for your service." The words came out without hesitation, and he followed them with a shrug. "We all have the things we're good at. Mine required a degree for validity, no?"

Wheeler's hazel eyes caught his. "You know...about that? I made myself go over all those emails you sent last night. They...uh. They were a little more helpful than they seemed at first glance. I should have read them sooner. So...thanks."

I should have read them sooner.

The look in Wheeler's eyes told him that was meant to be an apology, but also that they were about as close to the actual words the detective could manage. At least at the moment.

And he did get a thank you.

He answered Wheeler with a nod, letting himself accept the apology for what it was worth. Whether Wheeler liked him was beside the point. He required the detective's respect. "It's why I'm here. No one knows him like I do."

"No. I see that. I knew you were legit as soon as you mentioned that wedding ring. There are people on my team though that..." Wheeler rubbed the bridge of his nose. "We're all grasping at straws right now."

The temptation to reach over and pat Wheeler's hand was as surprising as it was strong. "He lives for that stress. He has to be getting access to it somehow." Adonai fed on it like a drug.

"If he gets off on it then he's getting feedback from someone." Wheeler's phone buzzed. After glancing at it he shoveled in the last of his breakfast, pulled out his wallet, and tossed cash on the table. "They've delivered the prison records and correspondence to you. You ready?" As Wheeler stood up he snagged the last piece of bacon and stuffed it in his mouth.

"I am." He left the toast untouched on the table. He'd totally forgotten that it had come. He wasn't here to eat, after all. He needed to find a killer.

Wheeler wasn't screwing around and hit a New York pace on the way back to the hotel. It was a short walk, made even shorter by the detective's determination not to lose time. When they keyed back into the room there were two boxes on the bed. Wheeler locked the hotel room door, ducked into the bathroom, then opened his closet.

Matthew let Wheeler do his job, focusing instead on getting his computer hooked up and online. His fingers itched to his get into the letters, but he knew he had to be able to think.

Really think so he could get back into Adonai's head.

"All good." Wheeler shrugged out of his jacket and tossed it on the bed; the black T-shirt that was underneath stretched across shoulders that definitely belonged to a marine. The detective removed the lids from the boxes on the bed and looked into them. "One of these is all correspondence and the other is copies of his records since his arrival. They sent everything. Some of it is on thumb drives, like his daily schedules, what he ate, who he met with, whether he was sick, physicals...tons of information."

"Good. That's what I need." He wondered if Wheeler had tattoos. He bet there were some. Marines got tattoos.

So did drunk grad students.

He slipped off his shoes, grabbed a box, and settled cross-legged on the bed.

He sat there for a second, wishing Ben was here to keep him from getting lost in Adonai's mind.

Wheeler stood beside the bed looking indecisive, then kicked off his shoes as well, dragged over the other box, and leaned against the headboard. "I'm not the fastest reader but I'm pretty good with details. What am I looking for?"

"Any sort of pattern. Anything that's out of a pattern. He's talking to the killer. I know he is." He started at the top of the pile, steeling himself to see that spikey handwriting. It looked evil. He would never admit it. Never. But he believed it.

Thankfully he'd grabbed the box full of letters because it was doubtful Wheeler could see what he would in them. Wheeler could look for the more obvious things: coming and going, dates things were received, diversions from normal routine.

"I agree. He has to be. Even if he didn't have to, he'd want to, I think." Wheeler pulled out a folder and started going through it. "People like that crave control, right? And order. He wouldn't want his gig happening without him."

"Exactly. He wants it to hurt. That's what he needs—anguish." He made himself start to read, letting himself slide down into darkness disguised by minutiae. Sorting the letters by topic, that was how to start.

The room went quiet.

Some time later, Wheeler tapped him on the shoulder. The sun had gone down, the lights were all on in the hotel room, and he was surrounded by paper.

"Hey, are you hungry? I ordered Chinese."

"Am I?" So many admirers, fans. So many people that wanted to touch evil. He was never going to eat again.

Wheeler blinked at him for a second. "Uh. Yes. You are. We skipped lunch. Let's put the paper down and let some of this stuff out of our brains."

Matt nodded, but bent back to the letters, eyes running over the handwriting. He was sorting by letter density. "Thank you for inquiring" didn't tell him much.

Wheeler's hand rested heavy and hot on one shoulder. "Hey. Matty. Take a break, man."

"What?" He blinked up, caught in between hell and purgatory.

"Food? Come on." Wheeler took the papers right out of his hands and grabbed his arm, moving him. "It's been hours. A lot of hours. You haven't said a word, had a cup of coffee, anything."

"I was working." He was busy, but now that he was distracted his stomach hurt, his back hurt, and his head was killing him.

He didn't even dare look at his phone.

"I didn't know what you liked. There's moo shu beef and chicken with broccoli and some spicy Szechuan shrimp... and my team came by with coffee and a flat of water." Wheeler actually sounded a little concerned for him.

"Thank you." He headed for the coffee, his stomach growling. "I love Chinese. I remember it being wonderful here."

Chinese food and pizza.

"Cool. Dig in." Wheeler started pulling containers out of brown paper bags and setting them out on the table, along with plates and chopsticks and forks and fortune cookies. "Usually I have beer, but I haven't slept in a while so that seemed like a bad idea."

"It could be unfortunate." Funny, but unfortunate. He'd bet a thousand dollars that Wheeler thought he was a teetotaler. He wasn't. At all.

"I do want a beer though." Wheeler sat in one of the two chairs next to the small round table and scooped some of the moo shu into a pancake on his plate. "Tell me what you've found. Anything yet?"

"He has a lot of fans—three in particular—that he

writes extensively. We'll start there." Once he'd searched everything, found the cipher, he'd figure it out.

"Fans. Fucking nutjobs. I mean I know it happens but... what is the matter with people? Men? Women?" Wheeler pushed a container of food toward him.

"Mostly women." They weren't doing this. He knew it. It was a man. He didn't know how he knew, but he did.

"I'd bet it's not a woman. Women kill people they know, right? And they don't strangle people. They prefer poison and things like that. I would bet Angie could tell me if she thinks the marks are a man's or a woman's hands. How many of those three regulars are women?"

"None. He doesn't answer the women. Not like this." And Adonai wasn't gay, didn't even seem to register men, on a sexual level. "These three get reams of response."

"Great. Do you want me to have my team look some of this over? More eyes?" Wheeler actually took his hand and put a fork in it. "Eat. So you can think. We need to think."

"Thank you." He stole a bite of broccoli. Oh. That was nice. "I like that. Anything unusual in your piles—breaks in routines?"

"It was a lot to keep track of, boring stuff like fresh air breaks and meal choices, so I started mapping out a timeline, going backward. I don't see anything yet, but I'm going to look at it again or...or maybe give it to you to look at, this is your thing I guess."

He nodded and stood, heading for the list, startled as hell when Wheeler grabbed his wrist.

"A bite of broccoli isn't eating. Sit, man. You need a keeper."

"Everyone says that."

"Yeah? Well everyone is right and so am I." Wheeler stood up, scooped some chicken and broccoli out onto a plate, then put his fork back in his hand. "I have a nephew. He's three. If I can make him eat, I can make you eat."

The words shocked the laughter out of him. "I eat a ton when I'm not working. I intend to fill a suitcase with bagels on my way home."

"Now you're talking." Wheeler sat back down again and refilled his plate.

Usually by now people had brought up Ben. He was surprised that Wheeler hadn't and wondered whether the detective didn't know—which seemed unlikely—or didn't know what to say. Or maybe Wheeler just didn't do the condolences thing. He wasn't so great with please and thank you after all.

Ben.

He closed his eyes for a second, remembering Ben—the bright eyes, the smile that lit a room. God.

He had to finish this so he could go home.

"So, I thought tomorrow you could meet the team, we could have breakfast or something. Put our heads together. Maybe actually do something besides talk about this guy."

"Okay." There was no way. He was staying in here and working. Doing his job.

Hiding and being safe?

Shut up, Ben.

"Yeah? Okay. Good. Maybe we'll have something to work with by then. Something we can go after."

"I'll do my best." He'd figure this out, send an email when he did. He looked up, catching sight of his Ben for a split-second.

Wheeler was watching him. "This is probably hard. Doing this again? Dealing with Adonai."

Agonizing. "I can think of things I'd rather be researching, hmm? One or two?"

"Yeah. Now that you mention it, I could do without this shit too." Wheeler tapped his fingers on the table anxiously. "I don't like waiting to see what happens next."

"We try to break the code, we find his partner, and we smash his fingers." It seemed like a fair answer.

"Breaking the code sounds like your department. Putting him away is mine. Smashing his fingers might be a no-no, as ironic as that seems." Wheeler stood up and started putting the food away. "I'm going to finish that timeline for you." The sigh that followed sounded tired and stressed, and the detective rubbed his forehead with one hand.

"Go home, detective. Sleep. I'll email if I find anything." He knew how hard this had to be. He remembered when sleep wasn't his enemy, when time wasn't his enemy.

"I don't know if I know how to do that; sleep when I know someone's life is in danger."

There were two beds in the room. "So, take a catnap. I'll wake you up."

Wheeler put the food in the mini-fridge next to the television. "Yeah? Maybe I could just close my eyes for an hour."

"Yeah. I'm safe. I won't hurt you." He liked the sound of a man breathing.

That made Wheeler laugh, and it filled the room for a second as the man stretched out on the other bed. "I'm not worried."

"I know." Too bad. Eventually Wheeler would be. Everyone was.

He took his coffee to the other bed and got back to work.

"Adonai is smarter than you are."

"Excuse me?" He glanced up sharply, glaring at Wheeler. But Wheeler's eyes were closed, and the man seemed to be sleeping.

"You're going to lose this time."

Matthew managed not to answer, but just barely.

He'll think you're sick, man.

"You are, aren't you? Sick?"

Ben. I need you. Please, love. He was so fucking worried.

You need sleep, baby. You've been up for days.

It was like Wheeler had said; it didn't seem right to sleep. His phone vibrated, reverberating on the wooden tabletop, making him jump. He reached for it and squinted at it, the black letters swarming on the backlit screen.

Are you okay? Text me back, please.

You should have let me come with you.

Hello?

Mari. Okay. Mari was worried too.

Hey. Here. Tired. Lots of letters.

Tons even.

But soon he could focus on the long letters.

What can I do? I should be there to help. You're eating, right, boss?

I had Chinese. Miss sopapillas already. He grinned at them, at how they knew each other's jokes.

I've been dreaming about eating everything bagels with my migas. Still think it'll be a day?

I hope so. He was afraid that he was wrong. Adonai was the most evil son of a bitch he'd ever known. His partner had to be close.

And what if he was smarter?

I hope so too. Call me if I can help. I'm pacing in your living room. Sorry. Mine was lonely.

Anytime, lady. Home soon, and we can talk. She was good to him, and he was so grateful for her.

Good. Be safe. Stay in touch.

Wheeler made a soft snoring sound and rolled over. It

was tempting to go over and pull the detective's shirt back down. It had ridden up, exposing the pale skin of Wheeler's trim waist.

He was pretty, and there was the hint of ink up on his back, maybe.

Matthew shook his head. There was no room for lovely things in the face of all this evil.

Ben was probably right; he probably did need sleep. He just wasn't sure he could.

The only thing he could do was dive back into the letters. It was the only logical answer.

If he was lucky, Wheeler would rescue him.

5

D erek gasped, eyes popping open wide. He didn't move at first but his eyes roamed the room frantically as he tried to get context. Where was he? What time was it? Was he okay?

Did anybody die yet?

The hotel room looked familiar and came back to him easily enough. He swallowed and sat up, feeling stiff and just as tired as he'd been when his eyes had closed. He rubbed the back of his neck. God, he felt gross. He needed a shower and to brush his teeth. He needed coffee. Clean clothes. He needed to talk to—

Oh. Einstein.

He glanced over at Herrera, and he really couldn't tell if the man was awake or not.

Herrera was sitting up, papers surrounding him, waist-length black braid beginning to look a little fuzzy around the edges. The doctor looked like a damn statue, looked utterly alien in his turquoise jewelry and jeans, the dove gray button-down lived in and wrinkled as hell.

God, he loved long hair. Maybe it was his time in the

military or his current line of work, but most guys he knew had the high and tight, low-maintenance thing going on. Derek supposed he'd been too preoccupied with the case, too tired and in his own head to notice until now, but that long, thick braid was gorgeous. Herrera's whole look was so not-New York, it was oddly refreshing.

"You okay, man?" Derek levered himself off the bed and stretched, trying to make tight muscles relax.

Bloodshot eyes met his, and for a second, there was total panic, like Herrera didn't have any idea who he was. Hell, he wasn't sure Herrera knew who anyone was.

"Whoa." Derek held those eyes and hurried over. What the hell could Herrera possibly have read in those letters? He took the guy by the shoulders, hands tight enough to give Herrera something to focus on. "Hey. Seriously. Are you okay?"

"He's sending out code, waiting for people to solve it." Herrera's voice was nothing but a croak.

"Code?" Jesus Christ. Herrera sounded as bad as he looked. And Derek got the feeling the profiler was altered too. High. He dove for the flat of water his team had dropped off for them, pulled out a bottle, opened it, and put it right into Herrera's hands. "Drink this."

"Thanks." The water went down in a couple of hard, painful-looking swallows, then Herrera pulled up a handful of letters. "They're all the same. Not word for word, but they're all the same code. He's sending out feelers to find someone to play with."

"To...play with?" Play? What the fuck? "What are you talking about? Three people are dead, Herrera."

Those black, black eyes met his. "Do you think he cares about that? Even a bit? The death of the victims—any of them—interests him not at all. It's about the emotional pain he can cause."

"You're not making sense. You're hysterical or something, man. Are you high? You need to slow down, back up, and explain this to me."

How long had he been sleeping? He rubbed his eyes and squinted at his watch. He hadn't actually looked at the time before he fell asleep, but it was dawn, or close to it and he was pretty sure is was before midnight when he'd closed his eyes. He'd gotten sleep...was Hererra not making sense or was he just too stupid to get it?

"Better yet, you need to come to the precinct and explain it to my team so we can get on it."

"What about this is difficult to understand? He's answered twelve of his 'fans' with basically the same letter." A letter was pushed over to him. "'Dear Bob, so lovely to hear from you. It was so charming to hear about your three dogs.' Three. Every third word makes up the message. So this one ends up as 'I'm eager to speak to you about making a plan. Please respond in kind. I have so much to teach you'." Another letter appeared. "'Dear Jim, so lovely to hear from you. I've never had the pleasure of two women at the same time.' This one is negative, so every other word going backward from the bottom—'Sincerely ready to speak to you about our plan. Respond in kind please. We have so much to learn.'"

He glanced at Herrera over the top of the first letter and then dug in, trying to work it out. These people Adonai was writing to would have to be fucking smart. Smart like Adonai himself. Brilliant even. Smarter than he was for sure, and that made him angry. And worried. It was one thing to catch someone bigger and faster and meaner. It was something else entirely when they were brainy and crafty and evil on top of that.

He stared at the letter, and for a while it just didn't work for him. But then, all of a sudden, he saw it. "Eager to speak...please...respond. So much...to...teach..." He looked up at Herrera again. "Oh God. It's not the same accomplice. He's found someone new."

"There's an accomplice. I know there is. But you're right. He has." Herrera looked...defeated.

Derek handed the letter in his hand back to Herrera. "Well which one is it? There are a dozen letters, you said? And you already found the three most likely yesterday. So which is it? Which one of these is the guy?"

"There's two possibilities—This one, Adrian Icko, and then Kai Caridon. I'm looking for their responses, as there's a significant correspondence. I'll call when I find it."

"Call." The guy really wasn't going to leave the hotel room. "You don't want to come brief the team?"

"Am I going to do more good here or there? You already think I'm high, and you've been with me for twenty-four hours." Matt didn't look like he was terribly worried about what Derek thought.

He raised an eyebrow and watched Herrera for a second. "You know," he said finally, backing off to find his jacket. "We're on the same side here, aren't we?"

"I came, didn't I? I have been trying to tell you. I could be at home letting the bodies pile up, hoping this time he stays close to home so I don't have to worry about my family."

Well, fuck. What was he going to say to that? He really couldn't imagine the horror of losing a lover at all, let alone losing one so violently to someone so evil. And worse, being asked to be involved with the same killer again.

He wasn't sure he could have said yes.

He stood there awkwardly, then gave up and decided that Herrera had earned the last word on that discussion. He pulled his jacket on and shrugged into the shoulders. "I'll wait for your call, then."

Herrera nodded. "As soon as I have something, you'll know. You have those names."

He watched as Herrera reached for another stack of papers. There were tiny paper cuts all over Matthew's hands, a fine tremor that only could be seen in the pages he held.

"You should take a break, get some rest." Even as he said the words, he knew they were ridiculous. He shouldn't have slept as long as he had either.

As he left the hotel he called the precinct, not sure who would answer for the team. He didn't want to start pinging people's cells individually in case someone was trying to get a little rest. He didn't head that way though; he was going to go home and shower first.

"Evers." Oh yay. Jack. Just who he needed.

"Hey, Jack. I have a couple of names I need you to research for me. You got a pen?" He wondered how this was going to go over, especially with him out of pocket since he picked up Herrera yesterday.

"I do. You survive Dr. Insanity?" Jack's chuckle was dark. "There's a pool going."

"I did. He's harmless. He's also a kind of brilliant I've never seen before." He flagged down a cab and got in it. "Write these names down. Adrian Icko and Kai Caridon. Both of them have correspondence with Rick Adonai that makes them suspicious. I want to know everything you can find out about them short of talking to anyone — no neighbors, employers, nobody. Just what you can find out without interviews. Got it? Get Leslie to help you and work fast."

"I'm on it. Spell those names for me?"

He did, and then he was alone in the backseat for a second, processing the last few days, the next few ahead of him.

He honestly had no idea what he was going to do next. He didn't like waiting, didn't like not knowing what was coming. He didn't like having to leave Matt alone in that hotel room either. Something about the look in those dark eyes made him worry.

Why, he had no idea. He wasn't a worrier. Not that kind anyway. He worried about this case, he worried about whether he could stay off cigarettes, but he didn't mess with people's personal lives, even if they were unexpectedly beautiful and slightly insane.

He didn't have time to be noticing things like that anyway, he finally had some leads to follow.

He got in the shower as soon as he walked in his door and picked up the trail of clothing when he got out. He pulled on clean jeans and another, similar black T-shirt. He avoided white or light-colored shirts because the ink on his shoulders was dark and tended to show through it. He didn't like being asked to pull his shirt off by people at the precinct; it was weird.

He couldn't believe Herrera had let him sleep all night, had managed to be still and quiet for hours at a time. The man had, though, and he knew that most any noise would have woken him.

Should have anyway.

These days he didn't know what was what.

He brushed his teeth and made himself a sandwich, then finally decided he was fit company again and headed for the precinct. He couldn't resist the urge to check-in on Matt though, so he texted from the cab.

How is it going? Are you okay?

Where are the rest of the letters?

What? *You have everything the prison system sent us.*

Tell them to fucking search again or I'll go rip the bastard's tongue out myself for playing games with me!

Adonai wasn't playing games with Herrera; that was ridiculous. Matt needed to calm down before he blew something. *We'll call and see if there is anything missing. Is there something specific you're looking for?*

Everything after 'come get me, Matthew, Ben misses you'. I'll text you dates.

He stared at his phone, tapped Matt's name, and made the call.

"What? I told you I'd text, *si*? I need to get the dates. He fucking knew I'd figure it. I want to read what he *isn't* letting us read!"

"It's personal now. I'm going to put a uniform outside your hotel room." Derek had a bad feeling that if Adonai was that far ahead of them, whatever the bastard didn't want them to read wasn't going to be read.

"*Mira*, look! Don't you dare. Call APD. Send someone to my house and protect Mari. He likes hurting me. Killing me won't get him off."

"Understood. Text me Mari's full name. I'll do both, okay? But you're now a witness as well as our profiler, and I have a job to do." He was going to do it right. By the book.

"I want every book, every scrap of paper, everything from his fucking cell."

Shit, he wouldn't want be the focus of that fury.

"I don't know if they'll let all of that go, Matt. I'm not sure that's legal. But I'll ask." His cab pulled up outside the precinct, and he paid the driver and got out.

"Get a fucking warrant if you have to. He's an active player in this game, and I need to know who the other person is."

Really?

He knew it was spiteful but part of him wanted to let the line go silent until Herrera said "please."

Emotions were running high, and that was forgivable when people's lives were on the line. In Matt's case, the even more tangible worry about losing people he cared about made Derek step back and breathe. "I'll do what I can, as quickly as I can. I'll set up that uni with the APD first, all right?"

"Thank you." The two words were honest, quiet. "I'll keep working. Let me know what you find out?"

"I will." He wanted to say eat something. Get some rest. But what he said was, "Keep in touch, please."

And then he hung up the phone wondering why it mattered so much to him. He wasn't the man's mother, and he had a killer to catch.

6

He read the same letters over and over until he could quote them, line for line.

Fishing.

All of them were fishing for someone to talk to, someone to play with.

And two men had responded.

Matthew put the two sets of letters side by side, exploring the differences, the similarities.

They began to meld as he stared, his eyelids so heavy.

He blinked then forcing them to focus when he heard male voices talking outside the door, and a second later there was a knock. "Matt? I'm going to use my key, okay? I'm coming in."

Matthew tilted his head. Really he should have locked the door, but he hadn't slept, so it hadn't seemed worth moving for.

As Derek opened the door, he got a look at the cop in a dark uniform standing outside. The guy was tall and blond and he wasn't sure the officer could get through the door without ducking. Once the door closed though, he focused on Wheeler, or tried to, taking in the ash-colored hair and the set of those strong shoulders.

"Have you even moved since I saw you last?"

"No." He'd been busy. Moving was a waste of energy. "What have you found out?"

"These guys are both bizarrely off the grid. We're working on it." Wheeler hovered at the end of the bed watching him.

"I was hoping you'd come and tell me one of them had blood under his nails." He knew better, but he was going for hopeful.

"I wish. I don't think anything about this is going to be that easy." Wheeler sighed and tucked thick fingers into his pockets. "ADP was very responsive. Mari is staying at your place with a uni outside the door, and I also asked them for an unmarked car to watch the building. They said she was a little freaked out when they showed up though."

"She's unhappy with me. She wants me home." He wasn't sure if he shouldn't send her to a resort in Guam to be safe.

"Is she...are you two...?"

Eee-a-la, Wheeler couldn't say fucking?

"Lovers? Committed? No." He rolled his eyes. "Gay. In that all the way at the far end of the Kinsey scale sort of way."

"Yeah, I can relate." Wheeler pulled a chair over and sat, putting his feet up on the end of the bed. "So, who is she then? A relative? She's very protective of you. She keeps texting me to ask if you're eating."

"She's my personal assistant. My family. She's a PhD candidate. We've worked together since..." Ben. "...for a long time."

Wheeler nodded. "Whatever you need for her, we'll do

it. Okay? I'm confident she's safe right now, but you just say the word."

"Thank you." He met Wheeler's eyes, blinking as he saw double for a second. "She's important to me."

"Yeah, I get that." Wheeler's hazel eyes were sincere, trustworthy. "She might be better off without you there right now, though. You know what I mean?"

"Maybe. If anything happens, I'll send her to my folks."

The room went quiet. Not surprisingly, Wheeler grew uncomfortable with the silence and popped back up to grab them each a water bottle, handing him one before sitting down again.

"How—you can tell me if this is off-limits, okay? But... how are you doing this? I mean, after losing your... I can't imagine. You don't know how much I appreciate what you're doing." Wheeler opened his water bottle.

"They tortured him. None of the others were. Ben was special." And that was that.

"Because Ben was yours. And you are smart, and Adonai enjoyed fucking with you. I read the file. And your emails are making much more sense to me now." Wheeler leaned forward and caught his eyes, looking right into him. "I'm worried you're going to get lost in this. Frankly, I'm worried you already are."

What did it matter if he was? Lost wasn't the worst thing on earth to be. Then he could stop hurting. "I appreciate it."

"How about you take a shower? And I'll get some food for you. Anything you want. And then you can get some sleep so I can stop lying to Mari."

"Sleep? But there's work."

"It's been three days, bud. For sure. That we know of. You have to sleep." Wheeler eased him off the bed and moved him toward the bathroom. "What do you want to eat?"

"Good pizza."

"That's easy. What do you want on it? You want some beer?" Wheeler stepped around him and started the shower.

"Pepperoni. If we were home, we could have green chile on it." He pulled off his shirt, sighing softly.

"I can—uh. I'll..." The detective looked away, at the shower, at the floor, then glanced back at him briefly and took a couple of steps back. "Gonna just...out here."

Wheeler disappeared behind the closing bathroom door.

Huh. He must smell bad.

He got in the shower and started washing, starting with his body and ending with his hair. By the time he finished, he felt like he was buzzing, like an electric current was running through his brain.

When he shut off the shower, he could hear music coming from the main room, and he'd know the smell of a real New York pepperoni pizza anywhere.

He shrugged into the terry cloth robe hanging behind the door, then he gathered his dirty clothes so the bathroom didn't look like hell.

The music was actually coming from the TV. Wheeler was sitting at the table, feet up on the other chair with a slice of pizza in one hand and a beer on the other. The detective raised the beer to him. "Pizza's here."

"It smells good. Really good." He nodded and took a piece. All of the papers were moved off the bed, the different piles carefully preserved, and he nodded his approval.

Wheeler winked at him. "I figured you were going to need somewhere to sleep, you know? Oh. Sit. I'll move my feet. Have a beer, man."

"Thank you." He couldn't have a beer; he'd crash, no question.

One appeared on the table in front of him anyway, and Wheeler popped it open for him. "How long does it take you to comb through that amazing hair?"

"About half an hour. That's why I keep it braided." It was his pride, his heritage, and his vanity.

"It's uh... I really... It's nice. That's smart." Wheeler sipped his beer and went after another piece of pizza.

"Thank you." He felt his own cheeks heat, but he hid it in the pizza.

"Mhm." Whatever Wheeler had been watching had really caught the man's attention all of a sudden. "Pizza's good?"

"God yes." He couldn't get pizza like this at home. Not even close.

Wheeler set an empty beer bottle on the table. "It's not professional I guess, but I just needed a beer."

"No judgment, man. If I thought I wouldn't pass out, I'd be all over it, but..." He shrugged.

"You need to pass out. You're wired, and you need some sleep. Even *your* brain can't do this forever. Drink it." Wheeler reached back across the table and pushed the open beer toward him. "There's a uni outside your door, and I'm here. You're safe."

"I'm not worried about me." Derek was in more danger than he was. Adonai wanted him alive. He took the beer, though, because the promise of peace was too much to resist.

"I am."

He was caught for a second in Derek's hazel gaze, the detective's eyes lingering on his longer than was necessary to get the point across.

"You have fascinating eyes. That's nowhere in your file."

Derek's lips twitched into the hint of a smile. "Somehow you managed to find out an awful lot about me. You've drawn some very interesting and accurate conclusions. I'm glad something is still a secret."

"Not anymore." Shit, he was a crazy bastard, but it was true.

Derek snorted and looked down at the empty beer bottle on the table. "That was a good beer."

He took a sip. Oh. Oh, it was good. "I haven't had a beer since—" Ben. "—a long time."

"I don't drink much anymore since I quit smoking. They kind of go together, you know?" Derek glanced up at him and then away nervously. "I don't even know why I quit. I hate not smoking."

"Cops, nurses, and waitresses." They were the ones that always seemed to smoke. He got it. He understood oral fixations.

"Cooks and dishwashers, cab drivers, construction workers, social workers, teachers. Everybody smokes. Not this cop though. Not in over a month." Derek reached for another piece of pizza, grinning. "I feel so healthy."

"Soon you'll be eating salads and doing hot yoga." He managed to keep his expression totally neutral, he thought.

Derek glared at him. "Namaste, asshole."

"The divine power in my asshole is an impressive thing." Wait. Had he said that out loud?

Whether Derek covered his mouth to keep from spitting out the pizza or choking on it, it was hard to say, but the bright red color was damn impressive, and the detective's inability to look at him was almost comical.

Should he apologize? Probably, but he didn't. It was funny. He'd been funny, once.

Derek finished chewing finally and went to grab another beer from the fridge. "Okay, that was funny, Matty."

"Don't worry. It won't happen again." And he wasn't a 'Matty'.

"I just didn't expect... I mean, you've been kind of...not funny, you know? It's cool." Derek sat down with his beer and took another bite of pizza.

He shrugged, but it was true. He was kind of not. It had slipped out. He blamed the sip of beer, the pepperoni without green chile.

"You look almost ready to—"

His phone buzzed. Someone was texting him. Like he didn't know who it was. He grabbed his phone off the bed.

There are cops outside the door, cops outside the building, they told me I have to stay at your place. Did you find something?

He knows I'm watching. You do what the cops tell you. You can stay on the third floor if you need to.

Let me help.

How? She was safest there, knowing the least she could. *I'll call you in the morning. Be careful.*

He could hear the sigh all the way from New Mexico. *Fine. Don't forget to eat.*

He shot a picture of the pizza and sent it. *Yes mother.*

"My keeper. She's unhappy."

Derek shrugged. "She gives a shit. I say go with it. Kind of rare to find someone that really cares these days."

He tilted his head. "Do you think so?"

He was lucky to be solely surrounded by people who cared, people he cared for.

"Definitely. Spoil her." Derek took a long sip of his beer. "Go to sleep, man."

"What are you going to do? I can work..."

"Try not to smoke?" Derek laughed. "I'm going to look at

those letters again and wait for my team to contact me with an update in an hour. If there's something you need to know I'll wake you."

"No smoking, I'm allergic. Pot, I can handle."

"I'm a cop. No pot." Derek winked at him. "But I don't have to arrest you."

"I have my medical card. At home, I'm legal." He grinned right back. "I use it for sleeping."

"Man, I have a serial killer out there. Do you think I give a shit about weed?" Derek laughed. "Just help me get this asshole."

The peace he was feeling dissolved with a pop. "He's counting on it. I will."

It would cost. Dearly. But he would.

Derek sighed and shook his head. "Yeah. Just get some rest, and you can get back to it when I have something for you."

"I don't think I remember sleeping." He dragged his fingers through his hair, working it into two quick braids so it wouldn't be in his way.

"It's like falling off a bicycle." Derek laughed. "Even you can do it."

The trails that Derek's laughter made fascinated him.

"That's the rumor." He only wished he could believe it.

Derek put his beer down, leaned back in his chair and crossed his arms, watching him. Just silently sat there, eyes on him, unmoving.

God, there was something intrinsically sexual about Derek, tempting, which was strange, given he didn't do temptation.

"Nightmares?"

He blinked at Derek. What?

"I'm trying to figure out why you're so afraid to just go lie down. Do you get nightmares?"

He'd seen his lover, his Ben, eviscerated, mouth a rictus of agony and terror. He hadn't been strangled like the rest. Ben had paid for all Matthew's sins. God yes, he had nightmares.

"I don't own a bed."

Derek frowned and leaned forward a little like he hadn't heard correctly. "You don't...oh."

The silence that fell then had a weight to it that he knew well. Derek was working out all of the implications of those five words. He hung a lot of baggage on such a simple statement.

When Derek looked at him again, that expression had changed. Softened in some ways and hardened in others. "I'm going shut them all down, Matt. End this for you."

He wanted to believe.

God, he wanted to believe.

He sat there, dazed, trapped in his own exhaustion.

Derek stood and approached him awkwardly, offering him a hand up. "You've got this. It's just a nap. Come on."

He blinked and took the hand, standing, ending up right there next to Derek.

They were close enough to breath each other's air for a second and then Derek swallowed hard and took a step back. "That's uh...that's a good start." Derek turned away headed for the bed, turned the comforter down and fluffed a couple of pillows. "Seriously. Beds are great. You're going to be fine."

"You're going to stay?" He wasn't sure if the words were out loud.

He got that frown again, the worried one. "Yeah. I'll stay."

Matthew slid the robe off and climbed into the bed, letting the sheets cradle his body.

Derek had turned around abruptly and headed for his chair again. "Sleep tight."

He wasn't sure if he could, but the sentiment was nice.

Matthew fought to keep his eyes open, but it didn't work. He had to trust in Derek to wake him when there was more work.

7

He was falling.

He'd gone right off the edge and was plummeting toward the earth at a million miles an hour, but he couldn't see anything but mist and darkness below him and—

Derek jerked awake with a gasp and looked around in a panic. He was in a chair. In a hotel room. Matt's hotel room. Right. Matt's fucking hotel room. He must have dozed off.

Jesus Christ.

The room was dim, but it had been dim before he'd dozed off so he couldn't have been out long. Just long enough to fall off a fucking cliff. Or...wait. Hadn't he thrown himself off? God, he couldn't remember.

No more beer, idiot.

He stood up and stretched and looked over at Herrera—Matt. They were kind of on a first name basis now, right? He looked at Matt who was lying still and sleeping hard. That was good. The guy really needed the rest.

He sat back down and put his feet up on the other chair, eyes still on the bed. Man, he'd thought Matt looked vulnerable sitting in the chair across from him. The way the guy was curled up right now made Matt look almost helpless.

And strangely beautiful too.

Which he definitely should not have been thinking. He shouldn't have been thinking a lot of things that he'd been thinking over the last few hours.

It wasn't strange that Matt looked beautiful. It was strange that he was even noticing things like that gorgeous hair and those deep, dark eyes. He'd never had this problem before with people he was working with.

But then he wasn't used to working with someone who had suffered the kind of loss Matt had. He couldn't imagine.

I don't have a bed... Had Matt really said that? The man was so scarred he couldn't even sleep in a bed alone anymore.

Matt frowned in his sleep, hand sliding over the sheets, searching. Derek shook his head knowing Matt wasn't going to find what he was looking for, and how much did that suck?

And then was standing by the edge of the bed, staring down at the reaching hand. He'd just gravitated there without thinking, drawn by something, by wanting to help. By wanting this to be over for Matt.

Derek reached down and slid a hand under Matt's, giving the man something to find. Something to hold onto and maybe help Matt stay asleep.

Matt's face relaxed, the frown disappearing. Matt's skin was dry, warm, and he found himself fascinated.

He sat on the bed and looked at Matt's hand, drawing his thumb over a knuckle and tracing the graceful length of one finger. It was just a hand, but it felt so intimate. Maybe that was because Matt was sleeping and hadn't really given him permission, or maybe because it had been a while since he'd just held someone's hand.

Matt sighed softly and stretched. "Don't let him find us, detective."

He should let that hand go, back off, walk away. He should probably feel embarrassed for being so forward, but he didn't.

"I won't."

He sighed. That broke one of his most important rules. He never promised anyone anything if he didn't have control over all the variables.

When Matt didn't pull that hand away, he curled his fingers around it and held on. He hoped to fuck that he could keep that promise.

———

"MATTHEW, you have to stop this. You're going to get hurt." Ben's voice was soft. Sure, though. Sure and firm.

"I have to stop him. I have to." He turned around, looking for his lover, for his best friend in the world.

Ben was sitting in window seat in the living room of their house, bright sunshine making his blond hair glow and casting a weirdly too long shadow on the hardwood floor. "No, baby. Your job is to help them do that."

"I should have... God. I should have been here to stop him." Guilt sent him to his knees.

Ben didn't move from the window seat, and his lover's calm expression didn't change. "You couldn't have. Even if you'd been here, there was no stopping him. It was good you weren't. There was nothing you could've done."

"I can't believe that. I needed to save you." And he hadn't.

He just hadn't.

"Please believe me, there was nothing you could have done, baby. I'm glad you're safe. That detective needs you more than he knows."

He sat there, needing a hug, a touch, something, and knowing he couldn't.

"I think you need his help too." Everything suddenly glitched like there was a bad digital signal—the entire room and his calm, smiling Ben with it—but not him. Ben said something else, he could see his lover's lips moving, but it came out garbled and he couldn't understand it.

"Don't go!" He stood up, panicked. "Please! Don't go!"

The whole picture started to fade, not to black but to colorless nothing. Ben was still talking as he faded, but the only word Matthew could make out was *love* before he was alone.

Matthew tried to breathe, but he couldn't remember how, he couldn't think.

All he could do was hurt.

———

Jesus.

Derek held onto Matt's hand, frozen and indecisive. What did you do for a guy that was shouting and crying in his sleep? Wake him up? Not wake him up?

He reached over and put a hand on Matt's chest, feeling the way the guy's heart was pounding. Derek felt like it was going to be ugly no matter what he did, and Matt was just... distraught. Panicking.

Wake him up.

"Hey." Once the decision was made Derek didn't hesitate, and rubbed Matt's chest harder, trying to wake him. "Matt. Matt? Wake up, man. You're dreaming. Matt. It's just a dream."

Those near-black eyes popped open, bloodshot and terrified, and for a second he thought Matt was going to attack him, but when the moment happened, no blow came. Matt just shrank inside himself for a second before Dr. Herrera was there, still bloodshot, still exhausted, but in control.

He hadn't let go of Matt's hand and he really didn't know what else to do to help so gave it a squeeze. "Nightmare I guess, huh?"

"No lo se. Did I wake you or no?"

Derek shook his head. "No, I've just been sitting here with you because you—" Because Matt...needed him? "I've just been sitting here. You okay?"

He saw it, that microscopic shake of the head. No. No, Matt wasn't okay, and he knew it.

"Thank you." Well, that wasn't the 'I'm fine' he was expecting.

He nodded slowly, eyes on Matt's, that darkness magnetic but so hard to read. "You're welcome."

"Would you like a cup of coffee?"

"I would. Would you like to get a little air?" They were going to go stir crazy sitting in here staring at each other and waiting on news.

"I've been outside more in the last two days than since... In a long while."

"Maybe that's a good thing. Fresh air helps me think." Derek got up, but he didn't let go of Matt's hand, using it instead to pull Matt up.

Then it got a little weird, and his cheeks grew hot, so he let Matt's hand go.

Especially because Matt was naked. Like nothing but

that long assed hair, Lady Godiva on her horse bare-butt naked.

He'd totally forgotten about the naked part, but not the hair. It was gorgeous. He wanted to run his fingers through it. Smell it. Feel it on his skin.

Jesus Christ, he needed to stop staring into the bottomless depths of those eyes and get the fuck out of this hotel room.

"So, coffee." Iced coffee. Snow and glaciers and penguins and anything but hot.

"Yes. Let me throw on some clothes."

Please.

Too bad he didn't know if it was *yes, please* or *please God, no.*

Where was his nicotine when he needed it? His palms were sweaty. What the hell was the matter with him? He wasn't going to let himself think inappropriately about the profiler, anymore. A profiler who, he reminded himself sternly, had lost a lover—*lost a lover, Derek. His fucking lover* —to Adonai, and now Matt himself could be in danger too.

He'd never been in his position before, this was totally new. And wrong. Totally unprofessional. Why the fuck did he quit smoking again?

Matt pulled on his boxer-briefs and jeans, that raven's-wing hair swinging. There was a tattoo of a thunderbird— which shocked the hell out of him, but besides that, Matt was like living statue, carved from teak.

Derek did his best to look like he wasn't paying attention, digging through his phone in hopes of an email from his team. And he found one.

"They got the warrant." He looked up at Matt, trying to ignore the smooth skin, but not quite managing it. There was no avoiding those eyes, though. "Everything that isn't nailed down in Adonai's cell will be on a plane in the morning. A federal marshal is bringing it to the precinct."

"Good. There will be a hint in there."

But if Adonai knew they were looking...

Adonai definitely knew they were looking. More to the point the guy knew Matt was looking, and there was nothing Derek could do to mitigate that. Part of Adonai's MO was the fine-tuned, emotional manipulation of the profiler, and at some point, Matt's point of view, even his insights might become tainted enough to be useless. Matt had to know that too. "I guess we'll see."

"Yes." So straightforward. So practical. Just 'yes'. Christ.

He watched Matt watching him. "You should put a shirt on."

Matt's eyebrow winged up, but he shrugged on a shirt, disappearing into the bathroom, and when he returned Matt was back, buttoned-up and re-braided.

Awesome. Perfect. The hotel room was starting to feel very small.

"Ready?" Derek went for the door.

Matt nodded. "As ready as I'll ever be."

He heard that.

On the way out, Derek had a few quick words with the cop outside the door and told him to stay put. The last thing they needed was someone getting in while they were gone.

It was dark and a little chilly outside, and the street was pretty quiet. The coffee shop on the corner was closed, but the diner down the street was open so that's where they landed. Sitting across from Matt wasn't quite the same as being alone with him, but it was challenging. Thankfully, ordering coffee was easy enough.

When it arrived, Matt wrapped his hands around the mug, the heavy turquoise ring clinking on the ceramic. He'd never seen a ring quite like it—smooth, thick, the stones inlaid with ropes of silver.

Neither one of them had said a word to each other since they left the hotel, and he really didn't know what to say to break the silence at this point, so he decided to ask about it. "I like your ring."

"Thank you. My father gave it to me for graduating with my doctorate. It was a thoughtful gift, coming from him."

"You're close with your family?" Derek family was as close as everyone's jobs allowed them to be. He saw everybody on holidays, and they texted pictures around. He'd see his sister and his nephew in Jersey a little more often.

"Close enough. They live in Santa Fe. They worry. They don't need to."

He laughed. "No, nothing to worry about. You're just being toyed with and manipulated by a serial killer who is in prison and has a protégé and probably an accomplice somewhere in this city. You're fine."

And they didn't know about that stuff. But they probably knew Matt never left his apartment and was obsessed with Adonai. They had to know their son was still grieving too. "Parents worry. It's their job."

"That's what they tell me. Are you going to settle down and raise babies?" The question didn't sound ugly, just curious.

"No clue. I'm going to have to cross that bridge when the fog lifts. Nobody wants to date someone with my hours." On the one hand, he could see himself out in a backyard playing catch with a kid, but on the other he knew he was lucky he remembered to wipe his own ass most of the time, never mind someone else's. "I think I'd fail as a dad, honestly."

"Do you? I can see it. You care; that's the important part, right?"

"Is that enough? I thought you had to Know Things." He put a goofy emphasis on those last two words and grinned. "I'm not really an advice guy."

Matt laughed, and the sound surprised him. Damn that was pretty.

He chuckled in return. "You figured that out about me, did you Mr. Profiler?"

"I did. You're a good man. You let me sleep."

"You needed it." He swirled his coffee and took a sip. "So what else does your profile of me say? Other than I'm 'desperately' trying to fill Detective Martin's shoes, that is."

"That you wish you hadn't taken the promotion, but you deserved it and earned it. You're a good cop."

Well, shit. That was pretty fucking spot on. He was a good cop. And he liked being a cop. "If wishes were horses, right? Here I am. Not everybody thinks it was deserved, but I don't plan on fucking it up."

"Good for you. Martin thinks you'll do fine."

He stared at Matt. "Wait. What? Are you talking to him? He's off-limits; he's retired." Okay that was annoying. Maybe insulting. "You checked in with him about me?"

"He's one of my best friends. You don't get to tell me he's off-limits."

Derek rolled his eyes. Of course Martin was one of Matt's best friends. Of course. Fuck. He didn't know what was worse—that Matt was reporting to Martin on his job performance or that he now knew that Matt was doing it.

He sighed and sipped his coffee. Profile his ass. Matt probably got all the information about him from Martin.

"I haven't shared anything about this case. I haven't spoken to him since Christmas when he shared pictures of his new grandbaby, Angel." Matt met his eyes, and it was damn near inhuman, that calm. Compared to the truth—to that blind panic when Matt woke—it seemed...incongruous. "He was there when we found Ben. He is the only reason I'm alive today. He likes you. He thinks you are a good cop. That's enough for me to trust you."

He held Matt's eyes while he thought about what to say to that. It should have been awkward to stare for so long, but the darkness of Matt's eyes pulled him in every time they locked on him. Trust was important, but so was truth, and Matt had to know Derek could see past that cold calm. Still, he didn't doubt the words were true even if the lack of emotion wasn't.

"There are some people on my team who think I should put you on the suspect list." Derek didn't think that would surprise Matt much. Matt might have gone off the deep end, but he was still managing to tread water. "I disagree. I trust you too."

"Thank you. Why do you think he started again? Now? Adonai?"

"Now? It's been a decade. Ten years is an anniversary. But there might be other reasons, like maybe his original accomplice was in jail on something unrelated and just got out. Or maybe it has to do with why he started this in the first place." Who the hell knew? "Why did he start this in the first place, do you know?"

"He was bored. He gets a sexual release from torture. He was cool, calm, implacable."

Until Matt got involved.

The crime scene photos from Ben Uvalde's murder had been brutal, fury and blood smeared everywhere.

"But if he didn't act alone, did they kill together? Was

this other guy a lover maybe?" Something about that didn't feel right.

Matt shook his head. "He's not queer. Could it be a woman?"

"Didn't we rule that out? Women like slow, sneaky murder like poison." They were running in circles now. Where was his team? He needed to know about those two names. "We're chasing our tails here."

"We are. And that's what he wants." Matt rolled his eyes, the expression utterly charming, which was weird as hell. "Asshole."

"There are stronger words." He fought the urge to reach for Matt's hand, the one curled so tightly around Matt's coffee mug. He didn't understand the attraction at all. Matt's look was unique, nothing like anyone he'd ever dated.

Which is probably the attraction, dumbass.

That was it. Matt was just different, and different was interesting. He needed to get over it.

"The Marshall will be here in the morning and then we'll know more, right? Do you want to walk over to the precinct and meet the team?"

"I suppose I have little choice, no? They'll hate me."

Wow, the social phobia ran deep. "What makes you say that? We're getting along fine."

"You mean you haven't wanted to smother me in my sleep yet?"

"No, no." Smother, no. Smothering wasn't at all what he'd been thinking while Matt was sleeping.

And God dammit he needed to stop going there.

"I have to check my ego a bit because you're a hundred times smarter than I am, but no. I'm not feeling homicidal yet."

"I'm just good at seeing patterns, no? It's a skillset."

"It's not just that, it's drawing conclusions. You're good at putting pieces together. I need to be better at that." He could dig up anything. Making it all make sense was harder than he felt like it should be.

"You have tenacity. It's worth a lot. Why did you become a police officer?"

"Because I didn't want a desk job with the Marines, and it seemed like the next best thing." He shrugged. One concussion too many to be the pilot he'd wanted to be. They would have kept him busy, but he finished out his mandatory time and moved on. "Not terribly noble or anything, but it's the truth."

"Truth is best." Matt touched his hand, the caress featherlight.

He didn't encourage it, but he didn't pull away either. He liked the tingle. "It's not always the easiest, but yeah. I try."

"Don't we all." Matt chuckled, and that touch disappeared.

He waved a hand to get the server's attention and tapped the lip of his mug, and she was over in an instant with more coffee for them both.

"So... I'm sorry, I don't know whether it's impolite to ask or impolite *not* to ask about Ben."

"What do you want to know?" Okay, that wasn't a 'back off, bud'.

"Whatever you want to tell me. How did you meet? What did he do? What was he like?" They were both tired, both stressed, it seemed better to focus on good things.

"We met in rehab. He was working his way through school as a janitor. He was...kind, strong, gentle. He laughed a lot."

Rehab. Right, Matt had said something about that. He

wasn't going to push that button, though that didn't mean he wasn't curious. "What was he going to school for?"

"Fine art. He was a painter." Matt's smile was warm, less sad than he'd imagine under the circumstances. "He had a solid following in Santa Fe."

"Yeah? That's cool. What was his...uh. Genre? Style?" Derek laughed. "I'm kind of clueless about art except that I like to look at it."

"He was inspired by the impressionists and the southwest. Desert colors, but soft focus in all things."

He knew what "desert colors" usually meant even though he'd never been to the desert. He'd never been that far west at all. "Sounds beautiful. You got any pictures?"

"Of course." Matt took a few seconds to flick through his phone before he handed it over. The painting hanging over the fireplace was huge—blues and sands and peaches swirling together, the image hinting of a vast landscape.

"Oh wow, that's really...amazing. Beautiful. I don't think I've ever seen anything like it. Is this in your house?" He looked at it another second before handing the phone back.

"It is. I own five of his pieces. That's the one I love most. The others are in museums on loan."

"Wow, that's cool. Really. That's impressive." Derek sipped his coffee. "Seems like he was an interesting guy."

"I thought so. He made me happy."

It sounded like that was a rare occasion.

"That's a great thing to have." It wasn't long enough but it was something. The trouble with losing happy was all that was left was unhappy. He didn't really know what else to say but that.

He sipped his coffee as the conversation dried up, trying to let the silence be okay.

Matthew watched out the window, the dark eyes taking in everything.

He texted Jack to find out if there was anything new, and Jack called him instead.

"News?"

"No. These guys have to be in or near the city, right? But I can't find anything recent on either of them. Leslie is doing the facial rec thing but we only have really old pictures on one of them so who knows if anything will come up."

"Maybe I should have Herrera come in and look at whatever you do have?"

"If you think it will help. I'm frustrated. I need a nap, boss." Jack even sounded tired.

"We'll be there, shortly." Derek hung up the phone and looked at Matt. "We need you at the precinct."

Matt took a deep, slow breath and let it out. "Then that's where I'll go."

That was a relief. Derek nodded, and this time he reached for Matt, resting his fingers on Matt's arm. "Thank you."

Matt's eyebrow went up, but Derek got a quiet look, something that he didn't quite understand. "Let's go."

"Right." He pulled his hand back, pushed his coffee toward the center of the table, and led the way out. He was glad, he needed the air. "Sorry if—I just know it's not... because I did say you could stay in the hotel room but...well. It's just a short walk." *Jesus*. That was fucking eloquent.

"I'll walk with you. Just you, fair?" There it was, that hint of vulnerability.

"Fair." Matt's demeanor put him on high alert. He popped the thumb break on his holster, and walked shoulder to shoulder with Matt as they made their way to the precinct. He'd basically just promised Matt was safe with him, and he intended to prove it.

There wasn't a hint of emotion on Matt's face, just a bone-deep stillness. Derek didn't relax until they were inside and headed up the stairs toward the conference room where his team was set up.

"Jack's brusque but a really good cop. Leslie's young and seems sweeter than she is, but she's smart. Those are the two we'll see most. Angie is the ME, she worked with Martin for a couple of years too, but she was appointed after Adonai went to prison." He put his hand on the conference room doorknob and hesitated. "And everyone is exhausted."

"Of course they are. This is hell." Matt never ceased to surprise him—sometimes the man seemed utterly insensitive, and other times he was incredibly empathetic.

Derek opened the door and ushered Matt inside.

"Hey, boss." Leslie looked up from her computer and her eyes went wide as she stood up. "Oh. Mr. Herrera. Wow. Welcome."

Jack was asleep with his feet up on another desk, and she hurried over to wake him. Matt's lips quirked, but the motion was so quick no one not watching could have seen. Jack's shoes hit the floor with a thud, and he came awake like someone had turned on a switch.

"Well, I'll be damned."

Derek stepped farther into the room. "Leslie, Jack. Matt is here to help, so let's give him a desk. Jack, you want to show him what you've got and then you can head home for a while and get some sleep."

"Sure. Sure. You think you can catch this guy?"

"You mean before he kills another of my lovers?" Matt offered Jack a smile. "Don't worry. I'm single."

"Jesus Christ." Jack got up out of his chair and gestured

for Matt to take it. "The next one will probably be someone's lover, right? It was just a question."

Leslie shot Derek, a look and he held up a hand to keep her from saying anything.

"There's a chance. He doesn't seem to care. In fact, he wants to torture the victims; it's easier without a support system. He's not into children."

Jack glanced at Derek and he made a 'keep it rolling' gesture. Jack nodded. "So, the two folders on the desktop have what I've found out about those two names you gave us, which is practically nothing. They don't have jobs on the books anywhere, they don't own property, they don't have current driver's licenses. I did track down where the letters are being sent, and both of them do have PO boxes near Grand Central."

"I'm trying to see what I can do with the facial rec software," Leslie added. "But it's a no-go so far."

"Anything in common with the PO boxes? Numbers? Anything curious?"

"Numbers are 618 and 1806. The return letters to Adonai aren't sent from Manhattan though. One set is sent from Brooklyn and the other from Hoboken. That's uh... Hoboken is in New Jersey if you don't know."

Derek rolled his eyes but didn't chime in.

Matt went white—not pale, ashy like he'd been shocked badly. "Is there a way to find out when the boxes were rented?"

Oh, he needed to know what that look meant.

"Yeah, sure. I just need to contact the...hang on."

"I got this, Jack." Derek put a hand on Jack's shoulder. "You go on and get some sleep. I'll call and wake you up when we need you."

Jack nodded. "Thanks, boss. Grand Central."

"I got it. Get a car home, expense it." Jack looked like he was ready to fall off his feet. Derek got another nod and Jack left the room.

"Leslie, make that call. Find out when the boxes were last opened and by whom."

"On it." Leslie went back to her desk and got right on the phone.

Derek leaned against Matt's desk. "What's up?"

Matt stared at him. Simply stared at him, and Derek wasn't sure Matt was seeing him.

"Matt. Matt?" He reached out and rested a hand on Matt's shoulder, squeezing gently. "Matt. What is it? What do I need to know?"

"It's Ben. The day he...when he...when it happened. June 18." Matt blinked and swallowed. "Six eighteen."

It was Derek's turn to stare. "Six...eighteen. Matt. Jesus Christ." He didn't say it out loud, he didn't have to. They both knew that whatever Adonai did next, however many more murders were planned, ultimately the sick fuck was coming for Matt.

He squeezed Matt's shoulder again and nodded, then straightened up. "Leslie? Get me that name. Fast."

"You got it. Everything cool?"

Matt turned and nodded to her. "Fine. I just need more information."

"You see anything else about these guys that maybe Jack missed? He said they were off the grid?" He resolved to keep Matt busy, focusing.

"Off the—" Matt blinked. "I need paper. A pen."

"Uh." He looked around and Leslie waved a legal pad at him. He hurried to grab it.

"Here, Derek. Pen."

"Thanks, Leslie." He dropped both on the desk next to Matt. "What are you...?"

"Grid. Off the grid. The son of a bitch made puzzles for a living. Off the grid. What are puzzles without a grid? Rebuses. Cryptograms. Anagrams. Hide and Seeks." Matt scribbled the words furiously.

*Lick? Dorian? Rain...*what the hell was this?

All he could do was squint at the cryptic scrawl and wait for Matt to hit on something coherent. And legible.

"Anagrams... Motherfucker. First names. Dan. Don. Dirk —Adrian." Matt wrote out R-I-C-K-A-D-O-N-A-I and crossed out the letters in Adrian, leaving Icko.

"Motherfucker."

"Shit." He grabbed the pen and wrote out K-A-I C-A-R-I-D-O-N. "R-i-c...fuck." He tossed the pen down on the desk and paced away. "The names are fucking bogus." And so far, they'd been their only leads.

"The names are. The PO boxes aren't. Someone's checking them. Someone's paying for them." Matt sighed, rubbing the back of his neck. "He's still in jail, right?"

"He is still in prison. The Marshall will confirm that when we see him tomorrow."

Leslie sighed. "I guess you don't need me to find those names."

"No." He moved to Leslie's desk. "Get someone to set up video surveillance on those two PO boxes. Adonai had to know that's what we'd do, but we don't have a lot of choice but to play along for now."

"On it."

"And then go home, Leslie. Get some sleep. I'll call you."

Leslie looked like she was ready to argue, but he shot her a look. "Yes, sir."

Matt was on his phone, typing furiously, thumbs moving in a blur.

He waited, which didn't really sit that well with him since he was supposed to be running this show, but Matt was onto something, and he had bupkis, so he was going to have to wait.

He paced away and back again, away and back, watching Matt text a mile a minute. "Not faster just to call?"

"I don't want to talk. This works." Matt was barely holding it together. Derek could see the cracks.

He moved around beside Matt's chair and rested a hand on Matt's shoulder again. He wasn't good at...this. Whatever *this* was. This was Leslie's thing, support and...empathy. Derek had no idea what to do except be there and make sure Matt knew he wasn't alone.

Matt took a deep, shaky breath, but the tension eased under his hand. "Tell me this isn't about me. Again."

He could say that, but it would be a lie. Matt knew that as well as he did. "Not *again*, it's different this time. I think Adonai is obsessed with you. He's playing with you, trying to prove he's smarter than you are. Ultimately, I think you're who he is after." Ben was the prize last time. This time is was Matt.

"Fair enough." Matt put the phone down, face down, the damn thing buzzing and jittering on the table. "So, puzzles. This is all about puzzles."

Derek wasn't sure if that was the right thing to say or the wrong thing, but Matt sure shut down all that emotion fast.

"Okay, Crash. There's a team headed out to put surveillance in place, and I'm outta here." Leslie hesitated in the doorway. "I'll be back after I get a shower and some breakfast. You guys need anything?"

"No. Thanks, Leslie. Get some rest, we'll need to put our heads together tomorrow."

"Right. Night, boss."

Derek watched her go, watched the door swing closed behind her, listened to the latch click into place, and sighed.

Matt's phone buzzed again.

"Who is that? Your assistant?"

"Yes. My father's coming to take her, and they're heading somewhere safe. She's unhappy."

Derek's desk phone started to ring.

He groaned and headed for his desk. "Shit, okay. Tell them to leave their cell phones behind. Get new ones that aren't smart." He swiped the handset off its base and put it to his ear. "This is Detective Wheeler."

"You tell the bossy bastard no! I'm not going to just desert him!" Ah. The assistant.

"I've got him. He'll be fine. I agree with him. You need to go lie very low somewhere."

"He needs help, he needs support, and he needs his family."

"What he needs..." Derek sighed and sat down heavily in his desk chair, trying to stay calm and reasonable despite feeling like this whole thing was spinning way too far out of his control. "Look. I know you're worried about him. But what he really needs most is to not lose anyone else to this asshole. You, his dad...get away. Go somewhere safe. Stay there. You want to take care of Matt, don't give him anyone else to lose sleep over."

"This is so fucking wrong, man. He's lost so much already." She was crying, genuinely sobbing. "He's safe there?"

God, this was awful. Just...awful. "He has lost a lot. He needs to not lose you. If I can keep him in the precinct, he'll be safe for sure. If he insists on going back to the hotel, I will be with him every minute and will protect him with my life. That's my job. He's on my personal watch." He hoped that sounded...real. Honest. He wasn't good at platitudes, but he was good at truth. Matt was his responsibility.

She sniffled softly. "Thanks. He's...he's not as strong as he pretends, you know? He's just not."

"I know. But he's okay right now." That was...mostly true. True enough. "He's worried about his family, and I know you'll make it so he doesn't have to be, right?"

"Right. I'm going with his folks. His dad's here now, and we're heading off. Matt has the landline number."

"Great. Take care, okay? I'll arrange a private line so he can call in a few days. Don't call us unless it's an emergency." Okay. That was good. He didn't quite know how he did it, but he thought he'd talked her off the ledge. "Be safe."

"Be good with him. Feed him. Make him rest."

"Yes, ma'am. He's had pizza, Chinese, intravenous coffee, and a nap. I'm on it." It wasn't health food, but it was food. "Be good to yourself, look after his parents. You want to talk to him?"

"No. I'll just cry more. I was hoping you'd make him let me come help."

He knew that, but that wasn't what Matt wanted, and he wasn't getting in the middle of that argument unless he had to. "I will if I think we need you. I promise."

"Thank you. I have to go. Mr. Herrera's here."

"Talk soon. Take care." Derek hung up the phone and sighed. Hoping he'd handled that all right, said the right thing. He was so uncomfortable with the touchy-feely stuff, but he figured this time all he needed to do was follow Matt's lead.

He knew this had all been Matt's idea, and he knew Matt

had stopped arguing with her because he'd let his cell phone buzz and buzz and never picked it up. Matt needed some backup, and she needed someone else to say what Matt really couldn't explain.

He couldn't imagine the horror of walking in and finding someone you loved...eviscerated, tortured, and knowing you just didn't catch him in time.

Derek stood up and went back to Matt's desk. "She gets it. She's going with your parents. Tell me what you need."

"I should take a walk. See if he's watching me."

Oh, he didn't think so.

"No. No, you're not going to leave the precinct. You're safe here. We have work to do." They didn't need to see if someone was watching, Derek would bet someone was. That was enough for him.

"I—I don't know what to do next." He didn't imagine Dr. Herrera had to say that very often.

And Derek didn't like the resigned set of Matt's shoulders as he said it either. It was way too early to get discouraged.

"I don't either." He sighed and leaned against Matt's desk, searching his brain for something to keep them both focused. Busy. "Well. We've got what, four days now? Tell me what you're expecting. Do you think we can stop him?"

"I do. He wants to escalate. This isn't about a long-term game. This is going to be fast and brutal."

Brutal was bad. Fast was worse because they didn't just have to catch up, they had to get out ahead of Adonai and his...protégé? Accomplice? Both?

"Can we save this woman in the laundromat? Can we work that fast?"

"Are there any connections in neighborhoods? Street names of the other murders?" Matt talked and made notes, but Derek wasn't sure Matt was talking to him. "We can send him letters to the mailboxes. I can send a challenge to Adonai, see what happens..."

He didn't know of any connections. Jack had run all of that and come up empty. Sending letters, though... "You mean let him know you know he's fucking with you? Is that a good idea?"

"I have no clue. I'm flipping through possibilities." Matt sighed. "I think he knows. If I'm in his head, he's in mine, but he's not the killer. Not anymore."

Adonai was doing something behind the scenes though. He'd brought new brains in, found his accomplice, all from behind the country's strongest bars. He was clever. Smart. Smarter than Derek really wanted to think about.

He looked at Matt. "Send the letters. Start a dialogue. We need to trip him up."

"All right. Do you want them mailed from here? Hand-delivered?" Matt lifted his head and met Derek's gaze. "I won't let him see my handwriting. I'll do it in Word."

He held those dark eyes and nodded. "Right. Good idea." He felt like he was caught for a second, suddenly wanting nothing more than to lose himself in those eyes. It took real effort to look away, but he needed some space, a little distance between them so he could think.

"We don't have time to wait for regular mail. I'll deliver them. I'll make arrangements to put them in the PO boxes myself in the morning."

That was it, right? They couldn't sit and wait anymore. They had to make a move.

"You got it." Matt picked up his phone and started typing.

8

M att wasn't sure whether it was morning or night, whether he was hungry or full. His entire world was this white noise, this low buzz that never seemed to fade.

His only constant was—*Derek*—Adonai.

Derek finished reading his letters and set them down on the desk with a sigh. "I have no idea whether these will do the trick, but I trust that you do. It's kind of scary how well you know this guy."

"He's inside me. He stole my world." Matt stood up, the letters clear in his head.

"I have only two needs. Find me a fine hotel somewhere close by, and never wait long for human contact. I'll wear my red hat for my love."

Derek was watching him closely; he could feel those eyes on him like a touch. "What does it mean though? I don't understand."

"Find a hotel close and wait for contact. Wear red for love." It wasn't much, but what if it worked?

"You're asking him on a date?"

Really? When was the last time Derek had a date?

"Yep. I figure I'm going to find him, blow him, and then use him to get to Adonai. It'll get hot then."

"Shut up, asshole." Derek paced away from him. "I guess it's a better plan than no plan."

"I'm hoping the current killer thinks Adonai is going to send someone." It wasn't much of a plan, but it was something. This wasn't what he did. He looked at patterns. He didn't *do* things.

"Well then we will send someone. Leslie. With backup. It could work if the guy is gullible enough." Derek passed him for the third or fourth time, still pacing, and rubbing at his forehead.

God, he hated this. Hated it. "I'm going to the restroom. I'll be right back."

He had to do something. Anything that wasn't sitting under all these fluorescent lights and feeling like a moron.

"Out the door, hard left, on the right past the elevators." Derek pointed in the general direction, pulled out his phone and started scrolling.

"Thank you." He walked out the door, took his left and then opened the door to the stairs and headed down. He wasn't trying to run, but he needed some space. Some time out of the lights.

Maybe he wasn't as smart as he thought, maybe he was just a fool with a bunch of paper diplomas.

"Hey, Mr. Herrera." A cop in a blue uniform stepped in front of him as he headed for the front doors. "Going someplace?"

"Just stretching my legs. That's all." He needed to breathe and walk.

"Okay. Try the central staircase, it's a pretty good climb." The cop wasn't letting him by.

"Thank you." Goddamn it. He headed for the stairs and walked up, telling himself to calm down, breathe. He wasn't a prisoner. Derek was just overprotective.

The staircase narrowed as it got to the fourth floor and smoothed out into a landing and a familiar hallway. Derek was leaning against the wall by the bank of elevators, hands tucked into the pockets of his jeans. "Did you get lost?"

"Nope. I went for a walk. Did you call in reinforcements?"

"I might have." Derek's eyes were on him again. "You can't just walk out on your own, Matt. What were you thinking?"

"That I need to walk, think, get out of the artificial lights." He was a thirty-year-old man. He could walk.

"Alone?" Derek took him by the arm and steered him back into the office, closing the door behind them. "You've lost your mind. We both know Adonai is after you. You're the ultimate prize here." Derek hadn't let go of his arm. It wasn't a painful grip, but it wasn't incidental either.

"You think it will stop if he gets me?" He didn't think so, but it was a possibility. More likely that the son of a bitch would just torture him, which really didn't sound fun.

"Honestly? I think he'd rather chase the mouse than catch it. But he knows we're onto him, so he can't play for long." Derek caught his eyes. "Matt. Don't do that again. Please. I need to keep you safe, you understand? I don't think I could live with myself if—" Derek cleared his throat, hazel eyes searching his. "If…" Derek let go of his arm and paced away. "Just don't."

"Can we go somewhere else? Somewhere without the lights?" He could feel Derek's touch, still solid and hot.

Derek nodded curtly but didn't meet his eyes. "Hotel. No. They'll be watching that. My place." Matt wasn't sure which "they" Derek was concerned about, Adonai's men or his own. He was willing to agree to anything in order to rest his eyes.

He gathered his bag, his papers he'd been scribbling on, the notebook. "I'll follow you."

Derek grabbed his phone off the desk and opened the door. "Elevator this time to the second floor."

"I wasn't running from you, detective." He was running from his doubts.

Derek stopped and looked at him. "I know. I didn't think you were running at all."

Oh. Okay. He took a deep breath. "Thank you."

"This is just insane. I get it. But I can't keep you safe if you don't let me." Derek pushed the elevator button. "And I need to keep you safe."

"I just need out of those lights. They hurt my eyes. Don't they kill you?"

Derek shrugged. "I guess I'm used to them. This way." They got off the elevator, crossed the hall and through a plain door and down a narrow stairwell. "Back way out."

"Good to know." He'd remember this. For next time.

Derek snorted. "It won't help you unless you're with the right people." At the bottom of the stairs Derek pulled out a card and waved it over a panel on the wall and the door unlocked. "Come on. We can try your hotel first. I gotta run out with those letters in the morning anyway."

"That's fine. You can leave me there if you want. I won't leave. I won't do anything but work and watch TMC."

"Not gonna happen. If you're not at the precinct, you're with me. I can't... I have to keep you safe." Derek just kept saying that.

"You have to keep the public safe. I'm...a bonus."

"You are not. You're what stands between him and

winning. I can't keep them safe without you. And that aside, there are people who care about you. And I—you're... growing on me."

Matthew processed that, and a smile crept on his face. "Like mold?"

"Kind of." Derek snorted and he got a grin. "Maybe slightly less toxic."

"Just a touch." He managed to keep a straight face, barely.

A low chuckle followed him as he led Derek into the lobby of the hotel. "You smell better too."

"Oh, that's all good, isn't it? Better that I don't smell like I've been put away wet."

"Yet." The elevator doors opened and Derek shouldered him in.

"Butthead." Man, they were reduced to one-liners. That was either miserable or funny as hell.

But Derek didn't even have a line for him this time. They got off the elevator and Derek shook hands with the cop outside his hotel room door, a different one than had been there earlier.

"After you," Derek held the door open, but didn't leave him much room to get by.

They rubbed together, Derek's arm, his belly, and he took a deep breath as he passed. He wasn't sure what he thought he was doing, but he did it anyway.

Derek breathed in too, the sound rough, and locked the door behind them. Hot fingers caught his bicep. "You can explain it I'm sure. You're smarter than I am. It's the stress, right? High emotion, proximity. Imminent danger?" Derek held on, keeping them closer than they should be.

"Maybe we're just men." Maybe they were horny. Maybe they needed.

"Is that an acceptable excuse now?" Derek tucked the other hand under his braid and rested it on his nape, stepping close enough to threaten a kiss. "All you have to do is say no."

"I know how consent works." What the hell were they doing? Did he care? He didn't think so.

"I think I was asking you to stop me." There was nothing tentative about Derek's kiss. The man obviously knew what he wanted, despite the incongruous words. It wasn't rough, but it was needy, all of Derek's focus on Matt like he was trying to make the distractions and the noise disappear. Jesus.

He threw one arm around Derek, pure lightning shooting through his nerves in a way he must have forgotten because he wasn't sure he'd ever felt like he was zapped with electricity before.

Derek didn't let up and went after his shirt with both hands too, confident fingers moving as if they knew things he didn't know.

Matt blinked, eyes going wide as his nipples went hard like they were begging for Derek's touch. He had lost his mind, but it wasn't the first time.

When they were both shirtless, Derek pulled back, took a huge breath and studied him. One hand reached up and traced his hairline with a gentler touch, but it didn't last long. He watched Derek swallow hard, Adam's apple bobbing, and then look down, fingers going to his belt.

Matthew sucked in, giving Derek room, and Derek's moan at the sight of his belly rippling was fucking gratifying. He reached out to drag one hand down along Derek's side, feeling the solid mass of heat.

Derek moaned again at the touch. "Hot. Your hand. Like

fire." His jeans fell open and Derek's hands found his ass, pulling them close.

God, skin on skin was—Matthew couldn't think, and he didn't want to. He wanted to burn, just for a second.

He hadn't realized they were moving until his legs hit the bed and Derek pitched forward with a grunt, toppling them both and forcing him to exhale. The man was heavy, all muscle on a sturdy frame. Matthew was grateful when Derek pushed up on one arm but barely managed a breath before Derek was kissing him again.

He opened up, his eyes rolling back as Derek fucked his lips, stealing his breath. All he could do was hold on and touch—grabbing Derek's muscled ass, dragging his nails up the long spine.

When Derek finally let him breathe it was to tug his jeans down and off, taking his shoes with them, leaving him bare. He let Derek look his fill, hoping what he had to offer was what Derek wanted.

Derek seemed surprised and looked him over with a grin, then loosened his own belt and stripped. "So, people who don't leave the house work out a lot, huh? Damn."

"They told me exercise would help me sleep. I have a pool." It was little and enclosed, but it was one of the infinity ones where you could just go for miles and nowhere, all at once.

Derek was completely comfortable in his naked skin, and didn't have as much ink as Matthew would have thought a marine might. "They're probably right. There are other ways I think are more fun." Hot palms landed on his knees and slid slowly upward toward his hips.

"Crunches?" he teased, rolling himself up halfway.

"No, but that's a nice view of your six-pack." Derek

leaned over him and licked him, drawing a line along the ridge of muscle. "Mhm. Very nice."

"Fuck." He managed to hold the crunch, but not for long. His muscles trembled and he had to settle back as he gasped for air.

"That's a good word." Derek licked the other direction this time, downward and over one hip.

"It's all good." His eyes were wide, staring sightlessly at the ceiling. He didn't remember wanting. Ever.

"Mhm." Derek hummed against his skin and caught his prick in one hand. The touch was surprisingly gentle compared to Derek's kiss, fingers stroking, exploring, thumb working across the thick head.

His toes curled at the touch, and his breath caught as Derek's thumbnail burned across his slit. *Oh, sweet fuck.*

The fingers were replaced by Derek's tongue and Derek didn't tease him for long. His cock slid easily past hungry lips and found sweet friction along the roof of Derek's mouth.

"Fuck. Fuck. Fuck." He couldn't help himself—not his words or the restless motion of his hips.

Derek circled fingers tightly around the base of his cock and took him deeper, giving him wet heat and suction, between long, approving moans.

He couldn't believe this was happening, but it was, and he wanted it. Ben would have to forgive him.

The fingers around his cock never let up. There was a sudden, hot pressure as Derek pressed a thumb against his hole, and even more as Derek swallowed around him.

Matt dug his heels into the mattress, the spring inside him letting go with a snap. He shot so hard that a blanket of silence fell on him for a minute.

Derek climbed over him again and took a kiss. It was

haphazard and sloppy between their sharp, shallow breathing and his difficulty focusing, but it was more than an expectation of quid pro quo. Derek didn't seem to be in a hurry.

Handy, because his hands were clumsy, dragging over Derek's broad shoulders, keeping him close. When he put his brain back together, he'd be better.

But he could feel Derek against his thigh where Derek rocked slowly into him, so hot and hard. Derek played with a stray bit of hair that had escaped his braid, running it through curious fingers.

Matt reached down, exploring as he went for that heavy prick. He wasn't a selfish man, but more importantly, he needed to know. He needed to know what Derek sounded like, what Derek felt like, what expression would be on Derek's face.

"You're smoking hot, you know." Derek's eyes burned into him and he had to wonder which one of them was actually smoking right now.

What did he say to that? He hadn't felt hot in...a long fucking time. He felt himself start to blush, to burn. "Come here and let me touch you."

Derek nodded and moved alongside him, propped on one elbow. Those eyes never left his. "Better?"

He nodded, took a deep breath, and tried not to give into the panic that was hiding right behind his need. The need to touch, to give Derek pleasure was bigger than the stress. He reached out and dragged one hand down Derek's side.

Derek took his hand, guided it lower to the hot base of a thick cock and curled his fingers around heavy balls. "Mmm. Warm hands."

Fuck, he could ride Derek for hours, up and down, just

filled completely. He closed his eyes and focused on touching, on the heft of that heavy prick.

"Yeah." Derek's voice had gone deep, raspy. A hand reached for his chest to tease an already sensitive nipple, rolling and pinching it.

"Oh…" Oh sweet fuck, that was like—like—like nothing he'd ever felt before. Nothing he knew. Nothing he could process.

"Good?" Derek moved to the other one and did the same, watching him so closely, rocking into his hand.

"I—Good." His eyes flew open, Derek's face so close. "Huge."

He squeezed Derek's prick, measuring that thick shaft from base to tip.

The answering groan rose from deep in Derek's chest, a low rumble that filled the room and at the end of it, a sharp inhale. "Fuck. Matt."

He nodded, because yes. He wanted to fuck. And suck. Touch. Lick. Jesus, what was up with him?

Derek pushed away, and rolled off the bed, muttering under his breath. "I hope to fuck I have a rubber in my wallet. It would be embarrassing to ask the uni to go get some for us, huh?" Soft laughter floated over Derek's shoulder.

"I don't do embarrassed." He reached out, stroking Derek's muscled ass. So fucking fine.

"You don't have to work with this guy. Also, you're not risking getting fired." Derek bent over and pulled a wallet out of the jeans he's just stepped out of. "We're in luck." The little package landed on Matthew's chest and Derek was right behind it, that cock finding its way into his hand again.

"Exceptional point." He rolled to drag his tongue over

the tip of Derek's cock, eager for a taste. Oh. Salt. Bitter. Heat.

Derek hissed. "Oh, fuck." A heavy hand landed on the back of his neck, keeping him there.

He opened up and groaned as Derek's cock filled his mouth, stretching his lips wide. Fuck.

He supposed Derek could have been smug about that, but that wasn't what happened. Derek seemed to know, and didn't roll or even move really, letting him adjust, letting him have control of the moment. "God. You feel good."

"Mmhmm." He relaxed his jaw and slowly let Derek feel him, fill him, get ready to take him.

"Oh, man." His effort was definitely appreciated. Derek was making some amazing sounds—soft grunts and long moans—and couldn't quite get a deep breath. "I want to fuck you 'til you can't think."

He would sell his soul for that right now, and he found himself nodding and taking Derek down and down, swallowing around the tip of his cock.

"Shit. Jesus." Derek got a hand in his braid and tugged hard, his voice like gravel. "Ease up. Ease up, I want you."

That firm pull made him arch, his hips grinding against the sheets for a couple of hard thrusts, and he popped off Derek's prick to take a wild kiss.

His kiss was answered with real hunger. Derek muscled him onto his back, burying him with body weight, wet cock leaving a cool streak on his thigh.

"Please." He bit at Derek's lips, feeling like he was about to lose himself, and not sure that he cared.

Derek groaned and leaned back enough to find that little packet and glove up, then open a different one before offering him two cool, slippery fingers. His eyelids went heavy, and he panted, that stretch the finest thing he'd felt in years.

"Yeah. You feel that, don't you?" Derek's fingers twisted and slid deeper. "Want to make sure you're ready for me."

He felt it, and that little twist, that push? It made him bear down, muffling his cry with one fist.

"Damn. You try my patience though." While those fingers kept after him, Derek sucked at his collarbone, not hard enough to leave a mark, but hard enough he knew it was on the table.

He swore he felt every single pull in his nipple, in his balls, in the column of his throat.

Derek sat back finally, trading fingers for the gentle pressure of that heavy cock, just right there and waiting, and looked at him, eyes sliding over him hungrily.

"Need you." Matt's voice felt raw in his throat, damn near painful. "Now."

Matt got a nod and Derek bent forward, pushing inside a little at a time. The restraint made Derek grunt and a vein stood out in his temple. "Fuck, Matt."

Thick. Fuck him. He felt that in his fucking soul. His ass burned and it hurt so good. "Please."

"Yes." Derek exhaled heavily, then thrust harder and forced himself deep enough their bodies pressed together. "Christ you're tight," Derek hissed.

"Full." He pushed up into a kiss, shutting himself up when he wanted to moan and beg for whatever Derek could give him.

That kiss muffled sounds from both of them as Derek started to move, rocking them together with long strokes. Matt felt every single inch of Derek's prick spreading him, dragging along inside him.

"Fuck this keeping quiet shit. Should have gone to my

place." Derek's whisper was barely that, rough and rumbling like thunder as Derek's thrusts grew more powerful.

"Not great at quiet. Fucking close." He nodded, teeth sinking into his bottom lip hard enough to draw blood.

"Yeah." Derek's back arched and teeth bit into his shoulder stifling another of Derek's heavy moans.

That burn sizzled him, all the way to his bones, and he couldn't have held his orgasm for love or money. His balls emptied, leaving him grasping at Derek's ass.

"Yes." Derek shuddered through a strong climax, releasing Matt's shoulder to suck in air, rocking them together over and over.

He moaned softly, trying his damnedest to remember how to breathe. In and out, he told himself. In and out.

He might have figured it out if Derek hadn't kissed him and stolen what little breath he had. A heavy hand pinned down his hip as Derek tugged free, leaving him empty. Thank God his cry was muffled in Derek's lips. Otherwise the cop waiting for him would be breaking down the door.

The heavy hand on his hip became a gentle touch along his temple. "You good? You're okay?"

"We—I'm good. We may both be possessed. That's okay."

"Maybe." Derek laughed and rolled to his side, still breathless. "I'll take it."

Matthew started to chuckle, the lack of tension in his muscles making him feel airy, like bubbles were exploding on his neurons.

Derek kissed his shoulder. "I feel fucking amazing. You're insane."

"Yes. Probably. Still. Thank you. I needed that." Look at all those coherent words coming out of his mouth.

"Yeah. Me too." That was followed by a huge yawn. Derek threw an arm over his ribs and tucked into his side. "Thank you."

"Can we rest? It's okay?" He was already sinking, the arm around him heavy and solid.

"Mhm." Derek hummed at him. "It's okay. I've got you. I know the guy outside. We're good."

Matthew nodded and let it go. Let himself just chill, breathe, and sleep.

9

Derek woke slowly, the strange sounds of Matt's hotel room the first thing he noticed. The unit under the windows was whistling slightly and blowing cold air. Someone in a bathroom above them or below was taking a shower, and the water running through the pipes was loud.

He was stretched out on his stomach, one arm under his pillow, one leg stretched out and pinned down with Matt's warm weight, and there was a hand resting on his bare ass.

Yeah. So, that happened. It shouldn't have, but it had, and it was one of the best fucks of his life too. He couldn't even bring himself to feel guilty. They were fucking consenting adults, weren't they? He didn't regret a goddamn thing.

He'd regret losing his job if it came to that though. That he'd regret for sure. And he'd sure as hell regret it if Matt didn't wake up feeling as good as he did. But right now? No. Right now he was feeling well-fucked and happy.

It wouldn't last, he knew that. There was a marshal coming with a box of shit for Matt to comb through. There were those letters to deliver. The two of them were going to be mired in stress and bullshit in an hour or two. Tops.

Matt groaned softly, hand sliding over his ass. "You're okay. I won't let him get you."

He sighed, rolled up on one hip and smoothed a hand down Matt's side. "I'm fine, Matty. You're talking in your sleep."

Matt's dark eyes popped open, focused on him. "I was dreaming about you."

"Sounds like one worth waking up from." He reached for a strand of hair that had escaped the thick braid and wound it around his finger. "You okay?"

"I am." Matt held his gaze. "Are we going to pretend we didn't have amazing sex or are we going to do it again?"

Jesus. That look made his balls ache. "Again. Soon." He hovered close enough for a kiss but didn't. "And also pretend, but only in front of other people."

Matt never blinked, but Derek got an immediate nod. "Fair enough. Kiss me."

No need to ask him twice. He gave Matt that kiss, lips locking in tight, and tugged a little on the swirl of hair in his fingers. He could get used to the way Matt arched up into him, gasping at the pull.

He shouldn't, but he could. He might even let himself. What he couldn't do was get lost in this right now, though. He ended the kiss and pulled away. "We should shower, get back to the precinct. I need to get those letters you wrote to the post office ASAP."

Like he'd flipped a switch, Matt rolled up with a nod, moving to gather clothes and his phone. "Is there a conference room I can use to go over the information?"

"Yeah, there are a couple of breakout rooms." That was

cool; they had a job to do and were on the same page. "Can I hop in your shower?"

"Of course." Those focused eyes landed on him like a touch. "You smell like me."

"I'm not ashamed." He winked at Matt. "Just a little sticky."

"I'm not either, but if we get in that shower, I'm going to end up on my knees, and we know it."

"Promise?" Matt was right, his dick woke up to prove it. He took a couple of steps toward the bathroom. "You stay right there."

"Yes, detective. Right here." Was that a smirk? That looked like a smirk.

He snorted and headed for the shower, but he had to grin. He didn't get it, but then again he didn't get a lot of things. Like K-pop and people who put mayo on French fries. At least he enjoyed this.

He was still pretty sure this would make some psychological sense to someone. Think about all the war babies, right?

War babies. He was an idiot. He took the fastest shower on earth just to give him less time to think. When he got out, Matt was there, hair down and loose, the shiny mass begging to be touched.

That had to be cheating.

"Shower's all yours." *So you can take your gorgeous hair and your hot bod behind a closed door now, thanks.* He was glad he had an errand to run this morning, he'd be gone for a couple of hours in this shit weather. That should put a damper on...things.

"Thank you." He could watch Matt walk for miles. Preferably just like he was, right now.

"Your hair is amazing," he said just as Matt was about to

close the bathroom door. Derek blinked. He hadn't meant to say that out loud he didn't think.

Matt stopped, and he heard, "Thank you. It's important to me."

"I'd love to hear about it some time."

"After work." The door shut and he heard the shower start.

"After work, then." He rolled his eyes at himself and got dressed. Maybe he could sneak Matt home tonight... assuming they left the precinct at all. He did need some clean clothes. Maybe some deodorant. A real toothbrush.

A blow job.

Stuff like that.

He wanted to see Matt sprawled across his mattress. He wanted to hear what Matt sounded like out loud.

Fuck, he could jack off to that visual forever.

"Cool it, Crash," he said out loud, as if hearing it would give it more weight. It didn't. He forced his half-hard dick into his jeans and zipped up like he was putting the damn thing in jail for betraying him.

He still wasn't sure what had snapped inside him. He wasn't sure what had gotten into Matty either, but he knew they'd both needed it, bad.

So, they had a little colleagues with benefits thing going on? Who were they hurting? They had a job to do and they'd go work their asses off today. They had the same goal. And it wasn't like either of them wanted more, Matt had to go back to New Mexico when this was done.

Hopefully it would be done soon. And when it was, he might rethink this detective gig. He was way more cut out for the shit on the street. This stress was something else.

He looked down at his phone as it buzzed on the nightstand and could read Jack's text without picking it up.

The marshal is here with a couple of boxes. He's huge.

Derek snorted and scooped up his phone.

Herrera is in the shower. Be there in a few.

Bring bagels.

Will do. And a bucket of decent coffee.

I might forgive you for leaving me here with this stiff collar.

He laughed, thinking: *You don't know from stiff*...then started laughing at his own joke. What the fuck was he doing, fucking a consultant, a target?

Okay, this angel and devil on his shoulder shit was getting old.

Set the marshal up in a conference room. Herrera requested a quiet space.

On it.

He looked over at the bathroom door when he heard the water shut off.

And get me an appointment with the postmaster at Grand Central. Don't give him details.

Okay, that's a new one. On it.

He answered a few emails as he waited for Matt, and then he got another of those visuals that he'd pull out on a lonely night. Matthew Herrera, damp and naked, wet hair braided down his back.

He let himself admire, because why not? If Matt was going to parade around like that, he was going to enjoy the show. "I've been asked to stop for bagels and coffee for the team on the way in. If you're uncomfortable with that I can get you to the precinct first and run back out."

"It sounds fine. Bagels here are special." The simple words made him smile. Matt tugged on a shirt, leaving it unbuttoned as he bent to dig out underwear.

Jesus. That was definitely cheating.

"That ass is pretty special too." He'd muttered it, but he knew it would be heard. Shit, Matty deserved it.

Matt stood, but not before he saw the blush climb the back of those thighs, cover that perfect ass. Jesus Fucking Christ. There was no winning this one. He was going to have to decide which battle to let himself lose.

His fingers searched his pockets for a cigarette they weren't going to find, and he sighed.

Matt pulled on briefs and jeans, dressing quickly, easily. "Has it been long?"

He blinked at Matt. "I'm sorry?"

"Since you quit smoking. Has it been long?" Matthew put his rings on, slipped on his shoes.

"Oh. It's been three months and a thousand years. I keep wondering when I'm going to stop asking myself why I quit. If ever I needed a vice, it's now." He sat on the bed to put his shoes on.

Matty went to the window and stared out. "It's so different here. So tight."

He didn't stoop to the obvious joke this time. There was something about the way Matt was standing in the window that looked so uncomfortable it didn't feel right. Instead Derek went and stood behind him, looking at the same view over Matt's shoulder. "It is. You get used to it. I guess you miss home."

"I miss my house. The mountains. The sky." Matty shrugged, so casually. "The green here is gorgeous though."

"There's not a lot of it in this neighborhood, but the park is great this time of year." Matt was squeaky clean, and he was drawn in by the nutty scent of Matt's shampoo. He slid one hand along Matt's side and around to rest on tight abs. "You...you smell really good."

Matt moaned, one long, drawn out sound that was pure pleasure. "And you feel amazing."

He took a deep breath and exhaled, dropping his forehead to Matt's shoulder. "We have work to do."

"We do. Bagels. Coffee. Work." Matt met his eyes. "Then we'll talk."

Derek nodded and stepped away. "Okay. Bagels first. I could eat."

"Coffee. Coffee first." Matt winked and grabbed his wallet. "Crazy cop. Coffee first."

Derek laughed and pulled open the hotel room door. "Right coffee. I promised the team a bucket of it. After you. Morning, Steve." He nodded to the cop watching the room. "Mr. Herrera will be gone all day. No one goes in, not housekeeping, maintenance. No one."

"Yes, sir."

He hit the call button for the elevator. "Have a good day."

"Does he have a phone or something to do all day?"

He laughed. "He has a job to do all day. But he started shift at eight, so he'll be relieved before you get back here tonight." If they came back here tonight and didn't end up somewhere they didn't need to scream into pillows.

"You know what I mean. Staring at my door is boring."

"Yeah. It is." It was. He'd done it. "But the point is to pay attention. He'll be watching who comes and goes, listen for sounds inside...he'll be bored and not."

"Hrm." Matt stepped into the elevator with him. "I would suck at that job."

"You're stuck in your head, that's why." Matt was the type to notice every detail in something he read or a case file but could probably make it all the way to the coffee shop without realizing it was raining.

"Absolutely. It's who I am."

Derek wasn't totally sure that was all Matty was, not really. The man under him last night hadn't been all in his head.

He leaned close to Matty as the elevator doors opened. "Nah. You were out of your mind last night."

He loved how Matty's eyes went wide, nostrils flaring. "Was I? You'll have to see if you can do it again."

"I'm feeling fairly confident." He grinned and stepped off the elevator first. "Coffee. Bagels."

It was pouring rain and he handed Matt his umbrella. "I have a hood." Not like an umbrella really helped much in this weather. In a New York storm, it often rained up.

"Water is falling from the sky. Interesting."

Was that a joke? That sounded like a joke.

"On the east coast we call it rain. Come on." He pulled up his hood and stepped out into the weather. It was a short walk and the coffee shop was on the way.

Matt followed close, watching everyone like a hawk. Derek didn't see any fear, just pure curiosity.

Derek was amused by Matt's lack of New York umbrella etiquette but didn't say anything. He did take the umbrella from Matt when they got to the coffee shop though, lowering and shaking it out before they went in.

"At least it's not also freezing out there."

"True. We get our share of snow, believe it or not."

"I like snow, but it's such a pain here. It's not even pretty an hour after it's stopped. It's covered in road grime and garbage." He ordered a baker's dozen bagels, two cups of coffee for them, and a huge box of dark roast to go.

"Oh. That's..." Matt shook his head. "It smells good in here."

"Hungry?" He handed Matt one of the coffees. "Careful, it's hot." Derek took a small sip of his own and it went down just right. Hot and bitter. "Oh. That's what the doc ordered."

"Thank you. Coffee. Yes." Matt groaned, the sound almost—*almost*—sexual.

He handed Matt back the umbrella, flipped up his hood and grabbed the bag of food and the coffee in one hand. In the other hand he carefully held his cup, then pushed through the door and back out into the rain.

They were both pretty damp by the time they arrived at the precinct, but the coffee was still plenty hot. Jack took everything from him, and Leslie took Matt's umbrella. "You okay, Mr. Herrera? Not too wet?"

"Matthew, please. I'm fine, thank you. There are boxes for me?"

"Leslie, you want to grab some bagels and take Matthew to the conference room? I have an appointment at the post office."

"On it, Crash."

He looked at Matty, trying to not look like he'd fucked the man the night before. "You have my cell if you need me, Matt. I'll check on you when I get back."

"I'll be here. No worries. I'm going to figure this out and squash that bastard like a bug."

"I like that attitude," Jack said, and gave Matt a thumbs up.

Derek wholeheartedly agreed. "Me too. Soon, I hope."

"Come with me, Mr. H—sorry. Matthew." Leslie held out an arm, gesturing for Matt to lead her out of the room.

Jack took a bagel and got some coffee. "How did it go with Herrera last night?"

Derek almost laughed. Jack would have a field day with the real answer to that question. He picked up a bagel and pulled out a tub of cream cheese. "He's a wreck. He doesn't really sleep. I think it's kind of tough being the expert on this psycho and having lost a lover to him too."

"Yeah. Yeah, that's fucked up, man. Talk about personal..."

No shit. That Matt survived was a miracle in itself, but that he could still fight Adonai? *Damn.*

"Yeah. I wasn't real sympathetic at first, but when you see him..." The way Matty swallowed back emotion and buried the pain every time it came up. It would be in his eyes one second and completely gone the next. "We need to keep an eye on him. Make sure he's safe."

"You think it's about him. Herrera. All of this." None of it was a question. None of it at all.

He nodded at Jack. "No doubt in my mind. Matthew knows it too. He wants it over, but I don't know what that means to him. And I think Adonai is counting on us understanding all of this. He's had a lot of time to map out scenarios. I think he knows what we'll do and he's setting something up. I don't know how not to walk right into it."

"Maybe there's something in all that shit that will twig Herrera." Jack sighed. "Where do you want me?"

"I need you to stay right here and watch the phone and the surveillance videos. I'm dropping off some letters, and I'm hoping for a quick response. I'll be back in a couple of hours." He stuck the letters in his pocket and took his bagel and coffee for the cab ride. "Call me about anything. Any little thing."

"You know it, boss." Jack snorted and winked. "I've got you covered."

"Cute." He wasn't sure what the wink meant but he wasn't going to hang around and find out. "Just do your job, Jack."

Derek sighed. Back out in the rain.

10

It was noon when he found the first note.

The letter was stuck to the back of another, and Matthew spent a good hour separating the papers.

"Aren't you feeling old yet, Matthew? Aren't you tired of losing the game? Maybe you should stop playing and find a friend."

Matthew scribbled down notes.

Old. Game. Play. Friend.

The second note was scribbled in a margin of a love letter.

"You're losing time, Herrera. The clock is ticking."

Clock. Losing.

It took another three hours to find the next one, on the inside of an envelope flap, written in pencil along the line of glue. It was almost gone, but he could read it.

"How boring, this world is digital, and we're trapped in the world of paper. I own your soul. I took it when my razor sliced into Ben the first time."

Matthew closed his eyes. He didn't want Ben here with him. He didn't want his lover to know what he'd done. He'd wanted it, ached for it, even. And he wanted to do it again. With Derek who touched him like he wasn't dead.

"God, Ben. He's right. He stole my soul."

No. Look deeper, baby. He didn't get mine. He can only have yours if you give it to him.

"Promise?" He didn't care about his; he needed to believe that Ben was whole and happy, wherever he was.

I do. Don't hand him what he can't get otherwise. He's only got words, they're not real. Real is kinder. And closer.

"I miss you." And he did. Still. But he had work to do.

He wrote the words he needed to highlight along with the others.

Old. Game. Play. Friend. Clock. Losing. Boring. Digital. Trapped. Paper. Soul. Razor.

God, what did this mean?

The door to the conference room opened suddenly making him jump. "Hey, I brought lunch. God, the fucking weather. You hungry? Whoa."

He looked around at what Derek was gaping at—papers everywhere, stacks and scribbles and general controlled chaos.

"You've been busy."

"He's leaving me messages." He looked up, forcing himself to focus, to *see* Derek.

Derek moved a pile of paper and sat the food down. "Okay. Come grab a sandwich first, Matty. You look like you've seen a ghost."

No one called him Matty. "I may have. A couple of them."

"Yeah. I hear that." He felt the tension ramp up in the room the second Derek closed the door. Just that quick. "You okay?"

"I am." He shook his head. Adonai had been planning this to punish him. The endgame was to get to him.

"Work on that. It wasn't very convincing. Come on, sandwich." Derek opened up a container of potato salad, set out some chips, unwrapped the sandwiches and the pickles. "Boring but it's food. You want a bottle of water?"

"Please. I've coffee'd myself into an acidy stomach. And boring food is good. I live in the land of spicy food. Sometimes bland is called for." The longer he focused on Derek, the more he could release the dull horror that was trying to dig into his brain.

"Well, you came to the right place." Derek laughed as he pulled two waters out of a cabinet and set one down for him. "Jack's been watching the post office boxes. Nothing yet."

"It'll happen. It has to. I can't understand what he wants. He can't get out."

But Adonai could terrorize him, and that was what got the motherfucker off.

"Mm. The turkey is pretty good." Derek was chewing and flipping through his phone. "Was Leslie helpful, or did you kick her out?"

"She helped me organize, and then she got a call and had to go."

"Ah. Okay. I wonder where she got off to?" Derek took a scoop of the potato salad. "What do you need to tell me?"

"I found three direct messages to me. These are the words I found important in all of them." He pushed over his pad. "Do they trigger anything for you?"

Derek read them out loud, and then mouthed them silently. "Well, no. Some of them seem like they should though. And some of them don't seem to fit at all for me... Boring. Digital. Soul. Maybe paper? I'm mean some of them are fucking with you, right? That first bunch? But then they stop tracking for me."

"Yeah. His old game is crosswords. You do it on paper. You can do crosswords digitally now, right? Is that a thing?" It must be. Was that the thing? The connection?

"Yeah. Like Social Words. I play that on my phone with Jack. sucks at it so I always..." Derek stared at him. "Win."

"Can we...see this? Can I play? I'll play with Adonai's toy." He grabbed his phone, sandwich forgotten.

"Uh. Yeah." Derek looked over his shoulder as he scrolled through available apps. "There. That's the one I play with Jack."

"Okay. I'll get them all. He'll find me." He had to do this right. He owed it to Ben.

"Matty, you should finish eating first." Derek's hand landed on his shoulder, heavy and hot. The touch hiccupped his thoughts, and he looked away from his phone. "You haven't finished your sandwich. I promised your friend I'd make sure you eat. I've already failed at sleep." Derek's laugh was warm, strangely affectionate. Not the professional cold distance it probably should have had considering where they were.

"That was better than sleep. Better than food too." God, Derek made him feel like he was...someone else.

"It was better than anything I've had in a long time." Derek's lips brushed his neck just under his ear. "A really long time."

His phone clattered to the table, tingles flashing through his belly. "Dios."

"I just need—" Derek perched on the edge of the table and bent to kiss him, lips meeting his with intention.

He pushed up, letting their kiss go deep and hard in a

single breath. Derek moaned, the sound vibrating over his tongue, and one hand tucked up under his braid.

His entire body felt lit up, electricity coursing through him in waves. He found himself achingly hard, his balls throbbing like he hadn't shot over and over last night.

They devoured each other hungrily and he knew Derek was wanting like he was, he could feel it in the way Derek pulled at his hair.

"Fuck," Derek swore, low on hot breath. "Fuck, I'm sorry." Derek pulled away and sat up, broad chest heaving.

"I'm not." He wasn't sorry at all. He was aching and breathless, but not sorry.

"Well, I shouldn't have—" Derek snorted. "Yeah. I'm not really either, except I'm sorry that we're...here."

"Yeah. Here is... Yeah." He'd needed it, though, that touch, that pleasure.

"Later." Derek reached out and covered his phone with one hand. "Two more bites and you can have it back."

"Butthead." Marissa must have talked to him. She did that to him all the time. It wasn't sexual when she did it; somehow that energy was there with Derek.

Derek shrugged. "Sticks and stones." Matthew didn't miss the deep tone or the way that Derek adjusted himself as he stood up, taking the phone with him.

He licked his lips and shook his head. He had believed, no question, that this sort of need was long forgotten. Still, the sandwich was good, and he managed to eat a good bit of it before he realized he might have been hungry.

"I don't like games. I don't think that way. I'm not good at..." Derek sighed. "Not that it matters. That's what we're dealing with, aren't we? There's only one truth here, right? If we don't win, we lose. There's really nothing in between."

"I'll win." He had already lost. This time he was playing for keeps.

"We, Einstein. We'll win." Derek handed him back his phone. "You're not in this by yourself, I think it's important you remember that."

"I know." But he knew that wasn't true. This was about him. This was focused on him. And his pain was the point.

Still, lip service was harmless.

Derek snorted again. "I said I wasn't good at games. That doesn't mean I don't know when someone is playing one." Derek pulled a pickle spear from the container. "He's your problem, and you're mine. That makes him mine too."

"I wish I wasn't sometimes. Good at playing games, I mean. It ends up horked somehow."

"I'm not going to let that happen again." Derek's tone was unequivocal. This time the man that was full of doubts seemed very confident.

"I hope you're right. I—I think I might need you to be right, Detective." Somehow it had become hard to breathe.

"Whoa. Hey." Something must be up because Derek moved quickly and pulled a chair up in front of him. "Matty. Look at me."

He stared into Derek, fighting to focus. He was fine. Just fine. Not panicking. Fine.

"Good. Breathe." Derek patted his cheek and held his eyes. "Ready? Deep breath in. I'm a fucking marine, Matty. I've got you. Breathe."

A fucking marine.

He heard Ben laugh. *Oh, amor. A marine? Look at you.*

"I'm sorry. I didn't mean to."

"Shh." Derek smoothed fingers along his hairline and under his jaw. "Just breathe. I needed to get your attention that's all. You're okay."

"I am. I didn't expect to see my name in his notes." And he hadn't expected to say that to Derek.

"You—" Derek stared at him. "Your actual name? Not some loopy game...it said 'Matthew'?"

He handed Derek the paper addressed to him. "It was glued onto another piece."

Derek looked at it for a long time, then set it back down on the table. "You better download that app."

"Yeah. All of them." Now Derek understood. He had to play. Now, before someone else died.

———

Derek had sent Jack home an hour ago and brought in a swing to sit and watch the PO boxes, but he had to wonder if it was a waste of time. Would Adonai use them anymore, now that Matty was online?

Matty hadn't found anyone yet in the games, despite using a couple of different and obvious handles, but they both knew he would soon. It was just a matter of time.

It had been hours though, and neither of them had eaten dinner or even left the room. Matty wasn't a machine, much as he tried to be one; he was just one slightly terrified man with a desperately important mission.

Derek hauled himself out of his chair and stretched. "Let's get out of here."

Matty looked up, and there was a dull horror in those dark eyes that Derek needed to erase, needed to dissolve. "Okay."

He'd been thinking food and coffee, but that look...now he was thinking better of that. Matty wasn't in any shape to sit in a room full of people and Derek could tell the man wasn't going to eat anyway.

But the hotel was...no. He'd take Matty to his place. He knew what they both needed.

"Turn the location setting on your phone off." His was already off, always was. He didn't need to risk being followed. "I'll take you home. To my apartment. Okay?"

Matty watched him for a second, then bent to his phone to change the settings. "I'm ready."

"Yeah." He gave Matty a quick nod. "Me too, come on."

He didn't plan on checking with anyone. Matty was his responsibility now and if Adonai wanted to get to either of them, he would. It didn't matter if there was a uniform posted outside the door or not, did it?

The rain had stopped but the dark sidewalk was still wet, puddles were reflecting the street lights, and the shadows were even darker than normal. "The city is neat like this. Right out of a detective novel."

He stopped at the curb and looked at Matty. Usually he took the subway, but he wasn't sure about tonight. "Subway or cab?"

"Subway is fine. I'm not claustrophobic. Thank you for asking." Matty wasn't in there, wasn't with him.

He'd accepted what was happening here, but he couldn't possibly know what it was like in Matty's head right now. All he knew was what he was feeling, and it was a weird cocktail of fear and determination, with a twist of a deep need like he'd never experienced before.

Hang in there, man. Derek would find him, even though he knew he'd lose control. It was okay. They just needed to be alone.

Matty followed him like his shadow had become a living, sentient thing, a too-tall silent Peter Pan.

It was late and the subway was quiet. He got Matty seated but he decided to stand close and protective, between

Matty and the aisle. The ride wasn't long, just silent between his own focus and how lost Matty was in his own head. It was kind of disturbing. Pretty damn scary actually, that someone could turn so fully inside themselves that way. He'd never seen anything like it.

"I'm close by, just a little walk."

Matty glanced up, looking around like he'd stepped into another world. "Good deal."

His building was well lit by a streetlamp right out front. It wasn't fancy, and it wasn't very big, but it was a nice place. Well kept up, decent neighbors...he could do a lot worse for sure. "Walk up, no elevator sorry. But it's only three floors."

"I live on the third floor too. No problem."

Wait. He thought Matty had a house. He started up the stairs, trying to figure out how to clarify without sounding like an asshole. "Third floor of what?"

"Pardon?" Matt looked confused. "My house. My assistant has the first floor, the second floor is communal space, and I live on the third floor."

"Oh. I get it." That sounded like a big ass house. "Communal space, like...what's it for?"

"I have a huge media room and a library, the pool is there, the sauna." So casual. The pool. The library.

"Sounds like a hell of a house. Did you have it built for you? Do you have land?" Derek keyed into his apartment, glad they were there finally, and safely. He locked the door behind them in true New York fashion, two deadbolts and a chain.

"I have ten acres, and yes, I had it custom built, but comparatively? The cost of living is tiny there." Matt looked around, taking his apartment.

"Here we just live tiny." His place was really small, and if Matty had that many acres and all that room, he figured it was going to feel pretty tight. But they had privacy, which was what he'd really been after. "You want a beer?"

"Do you have any Coke at all? Anything fizzy?"

"Sure. I'll get us Cokes." Derek wasn't sure if Matty wanted to settle his stomach or just not drink, but he understood either one. He pulled a couple of Cokes out of the fridge, gesturing to the living room. "Make yourself at home."

"Thank you." Matty sat, and suddenly he was struck by the strangeness of this. He hadn't had a man in here for a while. Definitely not one he wanted like he wanted Matt.

"Feeling a little better? I thought I'd lost you for minute there." Speaking was a step in the right direction, anyway.

"I am. It was—" Matt shook his head and opened his Coke, slugging it back.

Damn. "Insane. It's insane. He knows you're looking for him now, trying to connect." He—or they—were fucking with Matt, and there was nothing he could do to make that better. They needed to take these steps, let it happen so they could find a way to stop it all.

"He'll find me." That dull horror in Matt's eyes made him want to hurt something.

He put a hand on Matt's thigh and squeezed lightly. "He will, I know. But he'll find me too when he does." He held Matt's eyes. He couldn't guarantee that he could keep Matt safe of course, but he was completely committed to trying.

Matt's fingers tangled with his, and the man held on tight—both gaze and hand. "I appreciate it. I want you."

He nodded and stood, and gave Matt's hand a tug. He'd take Matt to the bedroom, see if they couldn't appreciate each other for a minute before hell broke loose. "Come on."

Matt followed, not a hint of hesitation in that lanky

body. In fact, Derek swore he could feel Matty's hunger pushing him.

He stopped near the foot of his bed, tugged his own shirt off, and tossed it on the floor before going after Matt's. "I want skin."

Matt nodded, hands on his belt, working his slacks open with clever fingers. Derek licked his lips and swallowed. He wanted a kiss, but he made himself wait. They didn't seem to have "just a kiss" between them and he wanted to pay attention, watch Matt move, admire.

He let Matt push his jeans over his hips and stepped out of them, stripping everything else off on the way. Matt groaned and licked his lips, eyes on his prick. Fuck, that gaze made him shiver.

He reached for Matt's belt and stepped closer. He felt like he should say something but didn't have any thoughts that Matt didn't already share. He lowered Matt's fly, the sound of the zipper enough to make his balls ache.

Matt's entire body went tight, tight abs rippling as he went up on tiptoe. Burning hands slipped up along his arms to curl around his shoulders, holding on as they breathed together.

"Fuck." Derek slipped his fingers around and under the waistband, hands cupping Matt's bare ass. He grunted as he pulled their hips together. "I'm trying, but I don't know if I have a low gear with you."

"I don't need low gear. I need you to fuck me so hard I can't think about anything but you."

Damn. That was direct.

And he could do that. Willingly. In a heartbeat. His mouth went dry, but he managed a raspy, "Get your goddamn jeans off then."

"Fuck yes." The clothes came off with gratifying speed,

that heavy braid swinging like a leash.

He'd tried to be focused on work, but he'd still thought about Matt all day. Fucking Matt was at the top of the list of things he'd had on his mind. The rest he really didn't want to have to think about either, so he took Matt's words to heart after he found protection and lube. He pulled Matt into a rough kiss, tongue pushing past Matt's lips.

One of Matt's hands wrapped around his cock, the other found his ass, and then they melted together.

Fuck yeah. He pushed his cock through Matt's fingers and groaned into the kiss. That braid was calling to him and he reached for it, weaving his fingers in and under the twists of hair until he had a good grip.

Derek explored Matt's mouth, finding the resistant length of Matt's tongue every bit as enticing as the soft give of his lips.

Matt fed him sounds that he'd never heard, wild and foreign, and his heart sped, his fingers tightened in the slick hair. Matt's grip around his cock firmed, bringing him up on tiptoes.

He broke off the kiss to suck in air. He wasn't going to wait any longer. He didn't have to, Matt wanted everything he did. "Need you. Now." He leaned in, using his weight to push Matt toward the mattress.

Matt met his strength, making him work for it, just enough for it to be hot, a hint of struggle that made it all feel naughty.

"That's how you are, huh?" A growl rumbled in his chest and he tugged harder on the thick braid. "Show me that ass, Matty. You know you want me."

Those dark eyes flared, the moment stretching out until the tension was damn near unbearable. Then Matt turned, offering him that sweet, taut ass.

He knew they were just turning each other on, but fuck if he didn't feel that much bigger for having won that little challenge. He reached for one smooth cheek and fondled it, fingers digging into muscle. "That's it." He kissed the little hollow behind Matt's ear, remembering how Matt had liked that earlier.

"Fuck."

Derek wasn't sure how Matt filled one syllable with so much need, so much emotion. The deep arch of Matt's spine pushed both neck and ass toward Derek's hands.

He let go of Matt's hair and ass and slid his hands down to Matt's hips, holding on and rocking, cock finding friction between Matt's cheeks. "So ready for you."

Matt spread his legs wider, and then reached back and grabbed his ass and exposed that tiny, needy hole.

Jesus, that was a sight. He wanted that so bad his thighs were trembling. He didn't waste time, practiced fingers dealing with the rubber and lube. He spent a lot of time prepping Matt either, just lined right up, the man had made it very clear he was ready.

He pushed in, letting Matt feel it. That tight ring of muscles clamped down on him, and it stole his breath as Matt's body fluttered around his cock.

"Yeah." Their connection was the oddest combination of desperate need and huge relief for him—he wanted to savor this, but he was so fucking ready to tear Matt apart. He took his time for now, giving Matt a second to adjust but he wasn't going to hold back for long. In and out, slow and easy, at least until he was balls deep in Matt's body, his world flaring with heat. "You feel so good, Matty."

But he needed more. He needed to hear Matt.

He pried his fingers off one hip and reached for Matt's prick, offering a light touch, just enough to get a reaction.

And did he ever get one. Matt's body tightened in rhythm with his touch, the sensation like he was jacking himself off.

"Jesus." That was the end of his careful control. Derek let go, hands moving back to Matt's hips and he thrust in hard, picking up a hungry rhythm. His thoughts narrowed to his own need, and he let it build, focusing on Matt's deep heat.

Wild noises escaped Matt, the sounds muffled in his sheets. Fuck, those cries were his. He let every one of them push him as he took Matt hard and deep, making sure he was everything in Matt's world, not giving the man a second to think about anything else.

He wanted to make Matt lose it, wanted to feel Matt come, wanted to watch the man tremble.

After one thrust, Matt clamped down hard around him. "Derek! There!"

"Matt!" *Jesus. Tight.* Derek raked air into his lungs and stayed the course, pegging that spot again, determined to give Matt what he needed—hoping he could keep it together long enough. He tugged his aching balls back down, trying to hold out a little longer. "Fuck, yeah. I got you."

"Fuck. Fuck. You. There. Gonna. There." *There.* That was it. That was what he wanted.

"Yes. With you. Fuck." One more second. He only had to wait a second more. "Now."

This time the cry wasn't muffled, and he let it drag him along, Matt's orgasm evident all around his prick.

Matt's powerful spasms stole his breath and the sudden explosion of sensation overwhelmed him as he came, hips jerking wildly. He got an arm under Matt and held on tight, hoping that might anchor him as his vision tunneled and the blood roared in his ears.

One of Matt's hands covered his, held it against Matt's smooth, hard belly, and somehow that connection was fiercer than the fucking had been.

It felt right, it was exactly what he needed. He blinked his vision clear as he came back to the room, and dropped kisses up Matt's spine, finally resting his forehead between Matt's shoulders. "Damn, Matty."

"Probably, but it's so worth it."

Derek snorted. "Every goddamn second."

He hadn't quite managed a deep breath, and he still had that fluttery feeling in his gut. He wasn't ready to let go of Matt yet either. There was no point in trying to put pieces together, he just accepted and enjoyed it, whatever it was, determined to stay in the moment and keep his focus on Matt.

He closed his eyes and Matt slowly eased them down onto the mattress. His hand was caught between them, Matt holding him.

He had that feeling he should say something again. The silence between them made him feel that way. Like the way Matt held his hand, the quiet was intense. Instead of speaking he took a light kiss, grinning when it actually stayed light.

"There's a storm coming." Matt's words were soft, but not sleepy.

He nodded slowly. "Yeah. But not tonight." Derek kissed Matt again and squeezed his fingers. "Not tonight."

"Not tonight." Matt cuddled into him, a soft hum filling the air. "You're warm."

He shifted and slid an arm around Matt. "You're gorgeous. And you feel so good."

Matt chuckled softly. "You make me... I've never asked..."

"You still haven't." He laughed, tucking Matt closer.

"That was a clear demand. Not that I'm complaining."

"A demand, hmm? That's not so bad. I can be a demanding bastard." Matty had a great laugh. A real, happy sound.

"I can handle that. I'm into direct." Hell, he was into Matt in general. He gave Matt's braid a gentle tug. "Do you ever wear this down?"

"When I'm home. Do you want to see?" The offer surprised him. The ease of the offer surprised him more.

"I do, yeah." He slid a hand down the length of the braid as far as he could reach. "Can I take it out?"

Matt nodded, sliding the rubber band off the end before dropping the braid and letting him have his way.

Derek climbed over Matt to sit behind him and picked up the bottom end of the braid. "It's heavy, wow." He started carefully unraveling the plaits.

"I haven't cut it in years. I wouldn't know what to do without it." Somehow that felt like a secret between them.

"It's beautiful. I'm fascinated by it." He loosened the last few thick bits and he combed his fingers through it, playing with the waves and kinks the braid put in it. "Is it really straight when it doesn't dry in a braid? Or wavy?"

"Really straight." Matt offered him another of those warm, soft chuckles sounded. "Except for the silver hairs. They're different."

"I don't see too many of those." Derek drew both hands down through it, from Matt's nape to the very bottom, flattening it out as he went. It was heavy and soft, and strangely soothing to play with. The scent of this morning's shampoo hadn't diminished at all, flooding his nose, and he leaned forward and inhaled deep.

"It's pretty hot, Matty. I gotta say. Is it good to have people play with it? Do you like that?" He could see how maybe it was personal, maybe it might not be something Matt let just anyone do. Then again, he couldn't be the only person drawn in by it.

"I do." The curve of Matt's cheek went a dull red, and he remembered the way Matt arched, moaned at a tug, a pull.

He hummed, fingers gliding through the soft, thick length easily now. He was trying not to think, to stay in the moment, but he'd never been good at that and his mind kept straying to what would happen next. Not work—he'd put work aside pretty easily—but with them. It was absurd to even think about, he knew. He wasn't sure how there could possibly be a "them" beyond this case.

He wasn't sure why he was worrying about it. He wasn't the long-term boyfriend type of guy, and Matthew Herrera was most definitely in need of a keeper. Someone to fuck him, someone to drive him out of his mind.

Twist my arm.

He could be that someone for a while, no problem.

Derek's fingers strayed from Matt's hair to his shoulders and found the muscles there crazy tight. Not really surprising under the circumstances. Derek, dug his thumbs in, working the knots.

"Oh fuck." Goosebumps popped out over Matthew's skin. "Derek. I can't breathe."

Silly man. Clearly his breath was coming nice and hard.

He didn't let up, finding hot spots and working his fingers into them. "What do you mean, you can't breathe? It's just a backrub."

"I—" Matt panted harder, his head shaking. "I don't know."

How long had it been since Matty had relaxed, even for a second?

"Matt." Derek curled his fingers over Matt's shoulders

and held them there. "It's just your muscles letting go. You can breathe just fine. Are you listening, man? You're fine. Take a deep breath." He squeezed Matt's shoulders hard. "Matt. Take a deep breath."

Matt sucked in a wild inhalation, the breath sounding fucking painful, but the second one was easier, deeper.

"There. See?" He eased up on Matt's shoulders and went back to his massage. "No wonder you don't sleep. You remember how this works now, right? Deep breath in, and then just...let everything go when you breathe out. Try it. When you breathe out, you know, exhale? Just let yourself get heavy. Like you weigh a million pounds." He wasn't going to win any prizes for his technique, but he thought he got his point across.

"A million pounds. Yeah. Is it supposed to be so hard, relaxing?"

"I find it pretty damn difficult. Yeah." He laughed. "Unless some hot, naked guy is giving me a backrub. That would probably make it a lot easier."

Oh, that earned him another of those laughs. They were addictive, because they were so rare.

"Oh, that's much better. You should laugh more often." He found another knot and worked on it. "First of all, you have a great laugh. But also, it makes you relax whether you want to or not."

"I've laughed more with you than... I have in years."

"I'm good for a little comic relief." Derek thought he'd been good for a little more than that, but he wasn't sure how to talk about any of that. He moved his hands to Matt's lower back, fingers finding more tight muscle.

"You're good. Full stop." Matt bent forward, offering him all of the long line of spine.

"Thanks. You've been good company too. Don't forget to

breathe." He probably should take that advice himself.

"Breathe. Right." That visual made him want to beg.

"Right." He kept up the massage as he leaned forward and kissed one of Matt's smooth, bare shoulders. The temptation was real, and they were already naked so it wasn't like anything was out of bounds.

Matt groaned for him, the sound deep and soft, and he liked the thought that his kiss drew it out from the depths of Matt's soul.

Not thinking about anything but Matt was easier than he thought it would be. At this moment, the man was everything he could see, hear, smell...the only thing he wanted to care about. He swept the heavy fall of hair to one side and continued exploring with his lips and tongue, taking his time because he could, just because he wanted to.

This amazing song filled the air—a symphony of moans and hums and sweet little cries as he explored. There was nothing stoic right now, nothing stiff and stilted. Every second flowed into another.

This was good. It was different. It wasn't just about fucking, or getting off at all, it was really about Matt. He was interested, curious. More than he'd remembered ever being before. Derek shifted to one side and tried a kiss, and it was different too because it wasn't hungry, it was...just a kiss. Matt settled beside him, solid and warm, and it was right.

Crazy, but his gut knew what it knew.

"That's...a lot better. I think." He moved again to lie back in the pillows and waved Matt down to join him.

Matt curled into him, one hand sliding along his belly, petting him. "You make it easier."

Simple words, not such a simple statement. He nodded, and hugged Matt closer in answer. He wasn't going to suggest sleep, it would either come or it wouldn't.

11

Waking up with Derek was amazing. Waking up with Derek to a screaming phone saying there was a body in a laundromat? Less good.

In fact, it sucked.

"Hurry up, Matt."

He struggled to get his clothes on, but he was addled, his hair wild from falling asleep with it down. He had to look like a monster. "I'm trying!"

Derek was shouting orders to whoever was on the phone, too. "Do not go in. Just seal it off, back, front, however you can get in there, and wait for my team. And call the ME's office. And...what time is it? Jesus Fucking Christ. Make sure there's fucking coffee."

Derek hung up, stuffed the phone into his pocket and stomped into shoes. "They sent a patrol car. It's outside."

"Right." Did he look freshly fucked? He felt pretty well-reamed.

Derek looked at him and sighed. "They already know you spent the night here. Just take another minute for...hair. And things."

"Comb? Brush?" Things? What things? He hadn't gotten fucked in his jeans. He knew there wasn't spunk on them.

"There's a comb in the...my comb isn't going to make it through your hair. Hang on." Derek disappeared into the bathroom and returned with a hairbrush. "I—don't ask."

"I won't." He brushed his hair out, groaning at the static. He managed to get it braided and to run a razor over his face. "Better?"

"Yeah." Derek stopped him, kissed his cheek. "You were looking a little too well-fucked for prime time."

"I'm feeling it." He managed to hold his smile, barely. "I'm in for more, when you are."

That was clear, he hoped. He was flying a path that wasn't familiar, not anymore.

Derek's smile faded. "Someone's dead, Matt. While we were...we have to go."

"Right." Embarrassment stung him, and he forced himself to remember who he was and why he was here. He straightened his clothes one last time, assuring that his expression was empty, still. "Do you want me at the crime scene? If not, I'll head back to the precinct and get to work."

"I want you there. I need you to tell me what I'm not seeing. And why he's a day early. And why we couldn't stop him. I wanted to stop him." Derek opened the front door and there were two cops waiting on the front steps to escort them to the car. "I guess you've spent some time in the back of a patrol car, huh?" Derek got the door for him. "After last time."

"I have." And the embarrassment slid into utter shame. Because sleeping with someone, caring for them had killed Ben. And what? Someone showed him kindness and interest, and he risked them too? He slid into the car as soon as he could and checked his phone. *Come on. Someone talk to me. Tell me why you're early. Tell me why you jumped the fucking gun. I need to go home.*

The car sped off, maneuvering through busy rush hour streets.

"When we get there, I'll—" Derek was interrupted by his phone ringing and he answered it quickly. "Wheeler. What? Jack. Jack, slow down." Derek went quiet and the look on the detective's face was actually hard to read. "Yeah. We're almost there. Thanks."

Derek hung up the phone and knocked on the safety glass between them and the front seat. "You can slow it down guys. There's no vic. It's a hoax."

He blinked over. "What? What did you say?"

Derek sank heavily back in the seat. "It looks like a murder scene but there was no murder. The woman in the laundromat is made of rubber and plastic. It's a fucking hoax. A fake."

A fake.

"I need to see."

A fake?

It was a puzzle, dammit. Two post office boxes, letters, now a fake body. What did it mean?

"Fine by me. I sure as fuck don't know what to make of it." Derek sighed and rubbed his forehead. "I'm just glad no one is dead. I'm not cut out for this shit."

"Me either. I usually consult from the house." He typed in notes on his phone, telling himself his hands were steady, he was calm, cool, collected.

Derek's hand ghosted over his thigh, the touch so light and so quick he wondered for a second if he was making it up. "We're here," Derek said, and then the door opened and the detective was whisked off by his team.

He followed more slowly through the crowd that was

gathering around the police tape. What on earth were all these people doing out and about?

"You still smell like sex."

He stopped, taking a breath and letting his head tilt. "Do I?"

His phone was in his hand and he dialed Derek blindly, praying he was doing it right.

"Don't turn around."

The voice was too close. Close enough he could feel the hot breath on his neck.

"No. I won't do that. What do you want? Is Adonai helping you?"

"Don't you say his name, you whore!"

"What's your name? You want to be heard. What should I call you?" He searched the reflections in the window, but all he got was a lean man, bald, glasses.

"I don't know. Why don't you call me Master?" The voice was raspy, in that way that made him want to clear his own throat. "That's appropriate since you'll be on your knees soon enough."

"Are you responsible for this little show? Did your master know you are going off script?"

Derek had his phone to his ear, eyes searching for him in the crowd now.

Yes.

"You think you beat him, but I'm going to make sure you pay."

Like he hadn't. Over and over.

Someone touched him, grabbed his hair, and he jerked away, pulled back, the distinct point of a knife against his back.

"You're going to hear from me tomorrow. And you're

going to do everything I tell you to do. My knife is sharp. Your detective is pretty. Ben was once too."

Derek found him and headed toward him. Their eyes met and in that same second, the knife, and the presence behind him, disappeared.

He spun around, searching for the bastard. "Where the fuck did he go?" No bald heads. Hoodies. Hoods. *Look Matthew*. "Where did he go?"

"Matty. Hey. Are you okay?" Derek's hand gripped his arm. "Where did he...? He was bald right? I think I saw him. Glasses. Shorter than you are."

"He has a knife. He grabbed my hair." Where the *fuck* did the asshole go?

"A knife? Jesus. Come on." Derek tugged on him. "I want you back in the car."

"What? He knows. He knows where I was last night."

"So, you're being watched. All the more reason to get you safe." Derek was dragging him toward the squad car he'd just gotten out of. "I think this whole scene is all bullshit. Staged. It was set just to get you out in the open."

That he was sure of. The point was to hurt.

He went, sliding into the squad car, looking around at all the eyes looking back at him. He kept his face still, but the wheels behind his eyes were smoking, screaming as they rolled too fast.

Derek slid in next to him and placed a solid hand on his thigh. "You're okay. You need to breathe, Matty."

He nodded and checked his phone that was still in his hand. No one yet. Not yet.

"Hey. Crash. What do you want us to do here?"

Derek turned abruptly, hand disappearing from his leg. "Treat it like a break-in, Jack. They don't need us. Tell them I want prints run and if they find a note to get it to me immediately and not to read it. I'm shifting the focus. Mr. Herrera is clearly a target now."

"What happened?"

"I'll fill you in at the precinct. Wrap up here, and you and Leslie get back there."

"On it."

Derek turned back around and Jack closed the car door behind him. "I think the precinct is safest. Do you agree?"

"That's fine." It didn't matter. If they wanted access, they'd find a way. Adonai had proven that.

He started making notes about what the asshole had said to him before he lost it. Focus on the work.

"I'll have someone come do a sketch for us, maybe we can get a better idea who this guy is." Derek tapped the shoulder of the cop in the front seat. "Precinct, please."

"Yes, sir." The car started rolling, and Derek watched the whole scene until it was out of sight.

Matthew kept looking at every person, trying to decide if it was this person, that person.

"I couldn't hear everything. What did he say to you? What did he want?"

"He said I was going to hear from him tomorrow, and that I was to follow his instructions. He called me a whore, wants me to call him 'Master'. He threatened to cut you up." That was what he remembered.

Derek stayed silent and leaned back into the seat. Finally, he sighed. "I'm sorry. I shouldn't have taken you to my place. That was stupid."

"I'm sorry that I made you a target." Something in his jacket pocket vibrating, making him jump. "What the fuck?"

Derek looked at his phone. "It's not mine. Or yours." Derek caught his hand and held his eyes. "Careful. And put it on speaker."

"Okay." He reached in his pocket, trying to only put his fingers on the edges. He dragged his finger across to answer. The incoming call was from an unknown caller, and he knew without wondering that the passcode was going to be the date of Ben's death. "Hello."

Matthew fumbled for the volume buttons as a painfully loud, ominous mechanical sound filled the car. The buttons didn't work.

"Jesus! What the fuck is that?" Derek shouted over the noise. Between the decibel level and the tone, he could feel the sound in his spine and vibrating in his ears. "Turn it down!"

"I'm trying!" He turned the speaker off at least. He knew that sound. He wasn't sure how he knew it.

"They planted a phone on you to play noise at you? What the hell was that? A...a machine? A blender?"

He didn't know. He grabbed his phone and recorded the sound before it cut off. Dammit. God*damn*it.

He needed to get into the precinct, into the little room with all the paperwork. He needed to finish this so he could go home. Derek was right. They shouldn't have. It was insane, to involve themselves like this.

The car pulled up outside the precinct and Derek got out first, looking around before moving over to let him out. Derek hadn't said another word in the car, hadn't really looked at him either.

He kept quiet, not wanting to cause more damage than he already had, and when they got back to where he recognized, he cleared his throat. "Do you want me back in the conference room?"

"You tell me where you need to be." Derek's tone was surprisingly gentle. Maybe...emotional? "I'll make sure you're safe there."

"I'm more worried about you." He met Derek's eyes. "At least now I know how he's going to call, right? My present."

"He's not really after me. I'm fine. He just said that because he knows it will upset you. He's pushing your buttons, terrorizing you. I'm—" Derek didn't shy away from his eyes this time. "I'm worried about you. I...need you safe."

That was what they'd said about Ben. "Ditto. So let's keep each other whole. I want to take you to my house next." His words popped right out of his mouth, without his permission.

Derek stared at him for a second but the look softened into an affectionate smile. "Deal."

"Hey. Detective."

Derek looked away from him. "Jack. I need a sketch artist. Have them meet us in the conference room."

"Okay. Look, no one's been near those PO boxes."

"They're a dead end. Everything is a goddamn dead end. Find me surveillance on the laundromat. Someone had to have a camera on it, the street, the intersection. All night and all day. Up until...now."

"Now?"

"We saw someone. He was there."

"Oh. Shit. Sketch artist. On it." Jack took off.

"I only saw his reflection in the window." He knew the voice, though. It was like the asshole had been gargling razor blades.

"These artists are really good. It can't hurt to try. I saw him too for a second. He had glasses." Derek steered him toward the conference room. "I'd like our tech people to look at that phone."

"Of course." He handed the phone over, blinking as he caught his hand shaking. "What if he calls?"

"We'll just hope he doesn't." Derek took the phone, put

it in a pocket and took his hand. "Listen. This is pretty terrifying. I feel it too. We can fall apart later, but we can't right now, not tonight. Not yet, all right? I'm here, we're both okay. We need to get to work."

"I'm fine. I have no intention of falling apart." He had survived Ben. He could survive this. He'd seen his lover's intestines draped over the furniture like decorations. He didn't have to be told to work. "Let me know if he calls. I'll start making notes. See if there are any references to the terms Master in the correspondence."

Derek watched him, finally just nodding. "Jack will send the sketch artist in when they get here. I'll be back in a bit." Derek gave his hand a squeeze, let it go, and left the room.

You're not a cop, baby. You're allowed to be scared.

"Hush, Ben. I don't want to talk to you." He'd just asked Derek to fuck him hard eight hours ago. He was scared, but that wasn't for public consumption, or for Ben's.

It's not your job to take care of him, remember. He's supposed to take care of you.

Derek was a cop. It was his job to find this killer. Matthew was here because he was a blithering idiot, and he'd put himself in the middle of things, just like Adonai had known he would.

Listen to the recording, baby. Figure out what it is.

"Yes, Ben. I know." He chuckled to himself and played the sound again. Right. Listen to the scary sound and identify it because he was a fucking master of weird assed...

He tilted his head. He knew this one. He knew.

He sat the phone on the table and played it again, the sound vibrating on the table.

A drill.

It was the sound of a fucking drill.

12

"It's definitely hers, detective." Kelsi handed Derek the cell phone. "I've been over it, it's her phone, it's even her cell plan."

The woman they were talking about was the very first victim in the case. A woman who'd been strangled in the alley behind a theater after seeing a movie with her boyfriend. She'd gone to the ladies' room and that was the last time anyone saw her alive. She was found in the alley with her pocketbook, complete with her cash and wallet, but like the others, no cell phone.

"Was there anything on it?"

Kelsi shrugged. "No. Her Facebook, mail, texts, she played a couple of word games. Nothing weird."

"Word games? Which ones?"

"Social Words seemed to be the one she liked the most."

He needed to tell Matty.

"Thanks, Kelsi. I'm going to keep this for a couple of days."

"I'll note that in the file. Good luck, detective."

They were going to need it.

The thought of people dying because of some sick game Matty and Adonai were playing infuriated him. No. No, Matty was having to play. He'd thought at the beginning that Matty had been enjoying this, but it was a lie, a facade. Matthew Herrera was being terrorized.

That was deeply disturbing on a professional level, and he didn't have words for how it felt on a personal one. He didn't think he should look too hard at that right now, either.

He made his way back to the conference room and knocked before letting himself in hoping not to startle Matt too badly. "Kelsi had a lot to say about the phone."

Matt had put himself together at some point, that long braid smooth, yesterday's button-down replaced with a form-fitting Sesame Street T-shirt, little round glasses on his face. Glasses? Huh. "Tell me."

He leaned against the table next to Matt and told him everything he knew, from the details of the first murder and what he knew about the owner of the phone to the word games. Matt listened intently and he did his best to stay purely professional, but he really wanted to compliment Matt on the glasses and tell him how adorable he looked in that T-shirt.

He sighed. "Have you eaten lunch?"

"No. I found out what the sound is. It's a drill, More specifically a rotary drill."

"A drill? Does that mean something or was he just trying to make us jump out of our skins? Because that fucking worked." That sound was worse than nails on a chalkboard and painfully loud.

"It's going into concrete, I think. That's the squealing. Masonry, maybe."

"I don't get it, but I guess we will eventually. I gotta tell you, I'm at a total loss here. I don't understand any of this. If he's trying to confuse me, it's working." He couldn't tie any of this together, and he felt like a complete idiot.

"It's a puzzle. Once we figure it out, it will all make sense."

Hopefully they didn't solve the puzzle too late. Whatever 'too late' meant now. He handed the phone to Matt. "You should probably keep this. It'll be for you if it rings."

"Hooray. I'm going through everything with the words master and drill, just to see what's what."

"Okay. Put me to work. Actually. Let me order us some food, and then put me to work." *Or just come back home with me and let's forget about all of this. Couldn't we?*

He knew they couldn't. And Matt was so focused he thought maybe he was overstepping even thinking about it.

"Can I please have a Dr Pepper when you order?" The question was soft, a twenty-dollar bill handed to him.

"Yeah. It's on the city." He pressed the cash back into Matt's palm, fingers lingering there. "You want anything special?"

"Whatever your favorite is. I'm curious to know."

He was curious about a lot of things too. "How about sushi? I'll get us some sushi. And a Dr Pepper." And coffee. A giant vat of it. He walked over to the conference room phone and called Leslie, telling her to order sushi for the whole team. "And Dr Pepper. A six-pack or a two liter or something. Okay?"

"Yeah, okay. Is Herrera all right?"

"Sure. He's fine." Fine. He's being fucked with, stalked, and made a fool of, but otherwise was just fine. "He's in here trying to help."

Matt was head down with the phone in hand, pencil flying.

"Good. Jack and I are working with the sketch to see what we can come up with. Nothing yet, but you never know."

It was a long shot. He and Matt hadn't gotten a good enough look to get too specific, but they'd agreed on the details they did get so that was good at least.

"Thanks, Leslie. Let me know when the food arrives."

"Will do, Crash."

He hung up and wandered back over to Matt.

"What were you trying to say?" Matt muttered under his breath. "Mason. Rock. Stone."

"Construction?" He pulled up a chair next to Matt. "Like asphalt or sidewalks?"

"Could be. Those drills aren't cheap, and they're not common."

"If he's calling you tomorrow why fuck with you today? Just because he can? If that's all it is then these words are just more bullshit. Like the dummy at the laundromat." More smoke screen. More...lies.

"Where there any words on the dummy? Anything weird? Any objects?"

"No. Nothing on the dummy." In fact, the dummy had been sliced open and made to look like it had bled out. But he wasn't going to tell Matt that. No one was, they were under his orders.

"Huh. I wonder if the word 'dummy' is the clue..." Matt wrote that on another sheet of paper.

He'd hoped for a note or anything that would give Matt something to focus on, but instead the laundromat looked like someone had sprayed it with fake blood. It was a gory, horrific mess and not a bit of it was real. This guy, whether he'd gone rogue or was acting on orders, planned to make sure Matt didn't sleep ever again. And probably worse. He had to start running some interference.

"Probably not. That seems...juvenile. Dummy. I'd focus more on what he—that he took a risk today. Why would he do that? And this drill thing."

Derek thought it was pretty obvious actually. The guy was jealous. Why else make his next move a day early, the morning after he discovered, or at least suspected, they were sleeping together? Why call Matt a whore? Why come close enough to touch?

"Right? I hear you. Mannequin, maybe?" Matt looked up at him, eyes wide, somehow innocent.

He reached for Matt without realizing what he was doing until his fingers brushed across Matt's cheek. "Yeah. Mannequin maybe."

"I'm sorry if I made you a target." Matt held his gaze, worrying.

He shook his head. "You didn't. He doesn't give a shit about me. He's just using me to get to you. All this other stuff, it's all distraction and noise *meant* to worry you. Meant to get into your head. It's absolutely clear to me now." He cupped Matt's cheek and drew a thumb over full lips. "And it's working. I can see that. You need to find a way to not let him in."

"Hey, Crash, sushi is here. They sent it over pretty quick, huh?" The conference room door opened abruptly, and he yanked his hand back.

"Yeah. That's great." He gave Matt an apologetic look.

Matt nodded and almost smiled. Almost. "Should we go out and save my Dr Pepper?"

"Was that for you? I wasn't sure. I hid it under Derek's desk."

"Good work, Leslie." Derek laughed and stood up. "Your

Dr Pepper is safe! Come on, let's eat. She can't save all the sushi, and Jack's dangerous around food."

"Exceptional. Sushi is proof there's a higher power that loves us. I'm a huge fan." That was a great grin.

Okay. He wasn't sure if it was something he'd said, the promise of food, or the second they had for a quick connection, but whatever it was Matt seemed...better.

There was a ton of sushi in the office, his desk was covered in containers and chopsticks and little tubs of soy sauce and wasabi. He was pretty happy too. "Nice work you guys. You even saved me some, Jack!"

"Leslie told me I'd better." Jack grinned. "And she outranks me so..."

He handed Matt a plate and some chopsticks. "Dig in." He certainly did, finding a little of everything, and filling up his plate.

Matt was pickier, choosing a half dozen bites and his Dr Pepper, and finding a place to sit with the guys, polite and quiet.

He rolled his desk chair over and sat with everyone. "Sushi is one of my favorite things ever."

"Me too," Jack agreed, mouth full.

He laughed. "Food is your favorite thing ever, Jack." Jack would eat literally anything. He'd never seen Jack turn food down. Ever.

"Hey—it's less dangerous than sex these days, and you can't smoke anywhere anymore."

Even Matt chuckled softly, as they all cracked up.

"You should quit like I did. It's great." He didn't hide his sarcasm. It wasn't great. He hated it. He wanted a cigarette right now, in fact. He could almost smell the open pack going stale in his desk.

"Do you smoke, Herrera?" Jack asked, and Matt shook his head.

"I'm allergic, believe it or not. Literally allergic to tobacco."

"What does that mean? You break out in hives?" He almost laughed. It was a damn good thing he didn't smoke anymore if he was going to give Matty hives.

"Yes. I have an anaphylactic reaction. Smoke just makes me sick, but...yeah. If you rub tobacco on me, I get hives."

"Wait, that's right you told me. Guess I'll stay quit for a while longer." He popped a piece of spicy tuna roll into his mouth and didn't look over at Matt.

"Yeah. And don't kiss him."

His lips twitched. "You're the smoker."

"Right. I won't kiss him either. But I'm not into guys so..."

He glared at Jack. "How about you put some more sushi in your piehole, straight boy?"

Jack grabbed a piece of sushi and licked it, making them all gag. Leslie stared over. "Seriously? No wonder you're single..."

Derek leaned toward Matt. "Jack is our comic relief. More because he's funny looking than actually funny."

"Ooh, ouch." Jack laughed and popped the piece of roll into his mouth.

"He's got my back though. Leslie's too."

"Yeah. She's married, and I still have her back."

"Love you too, Jackie." Leslie stuck her tongue out.

Matthew looked at all of them with the strangest smile, a little bittersweet, a touch sad.

"I bet you miss your assistant." Derek asked Matt. "What's her name again?"

"Marissa. She's a PhD. candidate at UNM, a wonderful researcher."

Jack looked at Matt over his chopsticks. "Is she single?"

Derek rolled his eyes. "She's not your type, Jack. She's smart."

"Ha-ha."

"Uh...guys? Is this your guy?" Leslie was looking at her computer screen.

"Is...what have you got?" He sat his plate down and hurried over. On the screen was a video of a bald guy in glasses waving at the camera. "Where is that?"

"This is surveillance video from the laundromat late last night."

Then the bastard held up a handwritten sign.

Ben says he'll see you soon.

Derek looked at Leslie and shook his head, and Leslie stopped the video before Matt made it over. He took Matt's arm and moved away from the computer.

"It was him. Waving at the camera. Leslie, keep watching let me know if he comes back."

"You got it."

Matt frowned. "Just waving? What is his game? I don't understand."

The phone on the table started to ring, and Matt's lips tightened. "I guess that's for me. Speaker?"

"Speaker." He nodded. "Go ahead."

Matt answered the phone, hitting the speaker button. "Dr. Herrera."

That awful sound hit Derek's ears, and Matt hung up.

"What the hell was that?" Jack was on his feet.

"Matt? Sit down, Matt." He guided Matt toward a chair.

"A drill. It's a drill. A masonry drill." Matt muttered, and the phone rang again. "Do I answer?"

What would happen if they didn't? He wasn't sure he

wanted to find out. He reached for the phone and answered it again, on speaker.

"This is Detective Wheeler."

"I want to speak to Matthew."

The voice sounded impatient, so he met it with all the patience he could muster. "Dr. Herrera is indisposed at the moment. Who is this?"

"I want to talk to Matthew, you *fuck*."

Breathe, don't play his game. "What's with the masonry drill, man? It's really annoying."

"I will cut your balls off and suffocate you with them."

Lovely thought. He didn't look at Matt, he didn't want Matt's reaction to any of this. He stayed focused. "You can try."

"You'll scream. There's a recording of Ben screaming. Did you know? I can play it. It's amazing."

Matthew stood up, eyes like holes burned in a blanket.

Derek reached out quickly and hung up the phone. "I'm sorry."

"Let's get you somewhere safe, doctor." Jack stood and herded Matt toward the door, talking fast and hard, even as the phone started ringing again.

"Do not let him out of your sight, Jack. Not for a second. I mean it. Not a second."

"On it."

He waited for the door to close and then answered the phone again. "What do you want now?"

"I told you. I want to talk to Matthew or I will go out and kill someone right fucking now!" Listen to that scream.

"You do that, and you won't get to talk to Dr. Herrera at all. Ever. So let's talk. Give me something, and I'll get him for you. Tell me why you're doing all of this. What do you want?"

He looked at Leslie and mouthed, "Trace?"

She held up one finger and made a "keep rolling" gesture.

"Matthew."

Leslie stared at him, wide-eyed. He got it. That voice was ice-cold with a bitter rage, a possession, a fury.

Everything in him went cold but he pointed at her computer. *Stay with me Les. Focus. I'll keep him talking.*

"Why? Because he helped put Adonai away? You should have gone away with him, right?"

"Don't you say his name!" The roar actually made the phone vibrate.

He gestured to Leslie and she shook her head.

Dammit!

"All right. I apologize. Let's calm down, okay? How about you come down to the precinct?"

"How about you put Matthew outside, and I'll grab him?"

He laughed. "Okay. You're smart. I see that. Listen, how about an agreement? You can talk to Dr. Herrera, but you're not allowed to mention Ben, or anything about him. You do and I'll hang the phone up. Deal?"

Leslie was still shaking her head. What the hell did this guy do to his signal?

"Aww...is Matthew still broken? He's cleaned up well."

He didn't take the bait. He needed to keep Ben out of the conversation.

"Do we have a deal?" He didn't want to involve Matt but he had to find some way to keep the guy on the phone. They should have had a trace by now.

He picked up his cell and texted Jack.

Where are you? Matt has to come talk to this guy. Leslie can't pin him down.

Coming!

"I won't mention the ex. Don't worry. I want him focused on me."

"We're getting him. He's on his way."

A second later Jack came bursting through the door with Matt on his heels.

"I'm sorry," he mouthed at Matty and held out the phone.

Matt shrugged and took the phone. "This is Dr. Hererra. How can I help you?"

There was laughter on the line, sarcastic and hysterical. "Are you kidding me? How can you help me? Isn't it you that needs the help?"

"Well, if you'd like to give us your name and address, that would be lovely." Jesus, Matt could be a cool, sarcastic bastard on demand.

"I have an important message for you. You're special, you know that? You're going to get a phone call from someone very important tomorrow. And he's going to tell you to listen to me. He's going to tell you to do what I say. And if you don't? Then the next scene you and your fuck-buddy find isn't going to be a fake. And it isn't going to just look familiar. It's going to be familiar. He likes games. I don't like games."

"Are you talking about the pseudo-intellectual that's pulling your strings from jail?" Matt's voice was like dry ice blown into his ears, the dark eyes reminding him of the pictures of demons his mother had shown him as a little boy, warning him about what happened to wicked sinners. "Doesn't it disturb you, that Adonai can jerk you and make you dance from a cell in Colorado?"

Derek glanced over at Leslie who just shook her head at

him. They weren't going to get a trace. He gestured for her to keep trying anyway.

"Tomorrow when you get that phone call you won't be dancing, you'll be crawling, Matthew. Crawling to me. On your knees. And there won't be anything anyone can do about it."

"Okay, that's enough." Derek snatched the phone back from Matt. "You're finished."

Derek hung up the phone.

"Well that was entertaining." Matt turned to go, just this husk of a man.

Derek reached out took hold of Matt's arm to stop him. "I'm sorry. We needed the trace but—"

"What the hell, Leslie?" Jack growled at her and stormed over to her. I thought this was your gig?"

"He must have been calling...from the internet or something."

"From the internet?" Jack snapped. "Or *something*?"

"Screw you, Jack." Leslie pushed away from the desk, chair scraping on the floor. "I'm not a techy, I did my best."

"Shut up! Both of you." Derek turned back to Matt. "I really am sorry."

"Why? You didn't make me the target of another psycho. That seems to be a calling of mine." All the life had leached from Matt's voice. "I'm going to get back to looking for something useful until he calls back."

Derek let go of Matt's arm and watched him leave the room, but it didn't sit well with him. "You two. Get what you can from that phone call. Take it to the techs. Have them listen to the background. Anything. Both of you."

He yanked open the office door and strode after Matt, rushing Matt into the conference room as soon as he caught up.

"Don't do that." He kicked the door closed behind them. "Don't let him do that to you. It's what they want. Hey." He spun Matt around, took the man's face in both hands, and looked into those dark eyes. "Matty. Don't."

"Mira, look, I—I'm trying to keep it together." Matt stared into him, eyes dead and still.

He knew what Matt was burying now, he'd seen it—the heart, the wild beauty—and it actually hurt him to know it. He couldn't stand it. "You don't have to. This is insane bullshit and you don't have to be together at all."

"It's work, remember? Do you think he would have stopped if I didn't come here?"

"No. But Matt, this isn't work anymore. Not for you. You're the target now. Now it's... it's on me." He needed to keep Matt safe. Close. God only knew what tomorrow was going to be about, but somehow he had to put a stop to this.

"Okay. What's changed? What do we do different?"

What's changed?

Everything had changed for him in the last five minutes. He didn't just need to keep Matt safe, he needed to bring the life back into those deep, dark eyes. And the minute he began to understand he was feeling something for Matt, something stronger than their working relationship really allowed for, was the same minute that Matt shut it all down.

"I don't know. I honestly don't but I'll figure it out. I'll—" Derrek tightened his fingers where they rested against that smooth jaw and brought their lips together. It wasn't a hungry kiss; he hadn't intended it to be. It was deeper, he tried to say more than he was able to manage with words.

Matt closed his eyes, one tear falling from the heavy dark eyelashes. God help him, he wanted to wrap around Matt and fix this.

"I'll figure it out," he repeated, softly. He had no idea

how, he didn't even understand completely what he was up against.

And he hadn't figured anything else out, had he?

"We will." Matt took a deep breath, let it out slowly. "We will, and then I need you to promise, after it's over, you'll come see my house. That's fair, yes?"

"Yes. I'll need a goddamn vacation about then anyway." He tried to smile, brushed a loose tendril of hair off Matt's forehead.

"I don't know what to do. I always know what to do."

He took a deep breath and paced away from Matt, thinking. "Okay what do we know now? He thinks we're going to deliver you to him tomorrow, is that it? He thinks Adonai is going to call you and...what? Threaten you?"

"No. He'll threaten you. That's the pattern, isn't it? He thinks he has something on you."

"On me? There's nothing...what could he possibly have on me?"

"I don't know. Would you get fired if they knew about me? Us? The sex."

"Yeah, maybe. Probably." He shrugged. "So the fuck what? We're talking about murder here. He wants to get me fired that's fine. I'm not gonna put anyone's life at risk over that."

Matt shrugged, the frown deepening. "So what else? My family is safe. I don't have a dog. Do you have someone they can use?"

"Yeah." He stopped pacing and looked squarely at Matt. "You."

Matt stared at him, and he swore the air turned electric, as if he turned out the lights, he could see the lightning. He licked his lips, eyes narrowing. "So what do you suggest now, Einstein?"

Matty squinted back, and Derek could see the flat belly ripple. "You—I—You know what I want to suggest. I know you'll tell me I need to focus."

Yeah. Focus. He liked the way Matt focused. "Try me."

"I need you. I—I've never felt anything like you, yes? Never. I need more."

He took three steps to the conference room door and locked it, then three more to cover the short distance between them. "Never this good." He kissed Matt again, hands sliding up and under Matt's T-shirt.

Matt groaned and slammed their lips together, forcing him to meet Matt halfway.

Jesus. Matt was as hot for it as he was.

Derek leaned into the kiss and slid his fingers over Matt's chiseled abs and warm skin, letting himself be turned on, letting whatever wanted to happen, happen. It was only seconds before his dick was pressing tight against his jeans, straining hard and needy away from his body.

"Matt. Fuck." His throat was dry, his voice dark and raspy.

When Matt slid down his body and tore open his fly, it shocked the hell out of him, but when that blistering hot mouth dropped over his prick, any thoughts he had shattered.

He had just enough presence of mind to clench his teeth together and swallow back his cry. That mouth was so fucking good it hurt, and everything Matt touched felt like it was going up in flames. He wrapped a hand around the back of Matt's head for balance and pushed his fingers into that thick braid, holding on tight.

Matt groaned and began to suck him like a fucking Hoover, dark head bobbing, working him like a master. His balls were tugged and rolled even as Matt swallowed around him, making him want to scream.

He tried words but he just didn't have enough air. Or enough brain cells. Hell, he didn't have enough anything. Matt was driving this train and all he could do was hang on for the ride. Heat was gathering in his belly, making his thighs weak, building behind a fragile wall that he knew Matt would easily demolish. Soon. Really fucking... *Soon*. "Fuck!"

Matt grabbed his ass and yanked, bottoming him out in that amazing fucking mouth and, literally, blowing his mind.

There was no hope, Matt just took from him. He'd been helpless to it since Matt shot him that look. He came so hard it bordered on painful, it made him shake, made his knees so weak it was a wonder he was still standing. For a second it felt like there was no air in the room.

Matt licked him clean, helping him through the aftershocks before tucking him back in and zipping him up.

"I swear to God, you're the fucking eighth Wonder of the World." Derek looked down at Matt, and although he was enjoying the view of the man on his knees, he offered Matt a hand up.

Matthew Herrera with fuck-swollen lips was quickly becoming his favorite sight ever.

He kissed those lips, then moved along Matt's jaw to his ear. "You want me?" he whispered. "You want to fuck my mouth, baby?"

Matt whimpered softly and nodded, hips thrusting restlessly against him. "Hard to be quiet when you touch me."

"You're going to have to be." He dropped his fingers to

Matt's jeans and opened them, lowering the fly slowly. "You think you can pull it off?"

"Oh fuck..." Matty stared at him, those eyes familiar now, liquid with lust. "I—" Matt bit his bottom lip, blunt teeth sinking in.

"You better." He knelt and teased a little, flicking his tongue out and tasting, testing what was left of Matt's patience, which he didn't think would be much. Matt rocked forward and he opened, allowing the needy prick to slide right in.

Matt stared down at him, eyes wide, and then that steady thrusting started, Matt taking him.

Derek wrapped his fingers around Matt's thighs and closed his eyes, letting Matt have him—wanting to please his lover, letting that satisfy him in a way he hadn't in a long, long time.

"I need you." The whisper was hot enough to blaze across his nerves.

He hummed, he could feel how the low sound vibrated through him and he knew Matt could feel it too. On the next thrust he sucked Matt in and swallowed hard.

"Gonna." Matty sucked in a wild breath, shoving one hand into his lips, muffling his cry, and he shot hard, balls going tight under Derek's chin.

Hell yeah.

He swallowed, feeling smug and teasing Matt's balls with one hand to make it last. He wished he could have heard that cry but knowing how hard Matt was trying to keep quiet was pretty damn satisfying too.

This was his, dammit. All his. And he craved it now. He let Matt go, dark eyes catching his as he stood. "Hey. You're beautiful."

Matt looked confused for a second before those cheeks went red. "Oh. I—thank you. I'm glad you think so."

"I do." He kissed Matt gently. "That was a first for me."

"You make me dizzy with need. Crazy."

"Yeah. It's incredible, right? Kind of insane." Derek kissed Matt again and then neatly put him back together— zipped up his fly, straightened his T-shirt, reached up and smoothed his hair. "Looking good."

"I don't know if I can do it, talk to Adonai. Not that and be Dr. Herrera, right?" There was a vulnerability in his Matty's eyes that burned him, and he'd do damn near anything to protect it.

"I get it. I really do." There were always options. He just didn't know if they were good options. "Okay. Well, what's your feeling? What do you think will happen if you just... don't? Will it be anything worse than if you do? What if we just don't answer that phone again?"

"He's going to kill again, but something has happened. Something's put the schedule off." Matt chewed on his bottom lip, beginning to frown, that amazing mind working. "What was it? What happened?"

"Has this nutjob gone rogue? He seems to be obsessed with you and not...not the way Adonai is." Adonai was interested in matching wits. This guy wanted something...worse.

"Maybe? It's perfectly possible. Serial killers can be unstable."

He snorted and couldn't fight his grin. That statement was as true as it was absurd. "You think?"

One eyebrow winged up. "A touch. No guarantee, but yes. I do think."

He laughed, tangling his fingers with Matty's. "I'm going

to remember that for future cases. Serial killers can be unstable. That's deep."

"I'm good that way." Matt rolled his eyes. "Fuck me raw."

"Been there done that." He grinned wider.

Someone tried to open the conference room door and slammed into it instead.

"Oh shit." He looked himself over, the room, Matt, then went for the door. "You good?" Everything looked okay. He yanked open the door and Jack practically fell in. "Sorry. Must have—uh. Locked. When I closed it. Sorry."

"I almost broke my goddamn nose." Jack glared at him.

He shrugged. "What have you got?"

"Brooklyn. Leslie thinks the call came from Brooklyn."

Oh. Whoa. "She has an address?"

"No. No, but I thought you'd want to know."

Looking for a random cell phone in Brooklyn would be a ridiculous waste of time. "Thanks, Jack."

"Brooklyn. Does that mean anything to you? Or is it just random information?"

Jack answered for him. "One of the PO boxes belonged to a guy in Brooklyn. There's an address but we checked it out, and it's an abandoned building. The whole thing is bogus."

"So he isn't close." Matty chewed his bottom lip some more, and Derek wanted to walk over and pull it out from between his teeth. "I was thinking if he was, I could go outside, make myself a target."

There was no way he would allow that. "Forget it."

"You don't think that's what that phone call tomorrow is gonna to be about? Adonai is gonna call him and tell him to turn himself over to that psycho on the phone today."

Derek stared at Jack. "That's not going to happen."

"It could happen if you get the bastard before he kills me."

"Did you just say 'if'?" He stared at Matt this time. Had they both lost their minds? "No. Out of the question."

"Boss, we could keep him safe, surrounded."

"He's a fucking civilian!" They were not dangling his lover like a cat toy on a string.

"Derek." Jack dropped his voice so low he had to listen. "What's the matter with you? We do this shit all the time. We put a wire on him, a vest—"

"Stop. Just stop, Jack."

"We'll worry about it tomorrow." Matt sighed, looking at his phone and shaking his head. "Nothing is supposed to happen before then."

Derek nodded. "Okay. Look. You and Leslie go home, get some sleep. We'll meet back here at nine. Keep your phones handy in case I need you sooner."

"Sure, boss. You keeping the phone?"

"It's supposed to be mine," Matt muttered. "I'll take it."

"No, I'll take it." Derek sighed, he was going to have to clear his head about Matt and think things over. "It needs to be with one of us in case he calls again before tomorrow." Hopefully no one did. Matt needed some sleep, he looked exhausted on every level imaginable.

"Have you considered taking Dr. Herrera to a safe house?"

"I have to go back to the hotel for clothes. I smell bad."

"I hadn't but he'll track that phone." He looked at Matt. "Can we leave the phone here overnight? Or will that just worry you?"

Matt stared at the phone for a second, staring like it would ring or explode from his will alone. "I—I've had— Can we just leave it?"

"Yes." Derek looked at Jack. Staying all night at the precinct was an option but the safe house was a better one for sleep. "Jack, I want you to go to his hotel, pack up his things and meet us at the safe house. Which one is open? Purple? Rainbow? Take Leslie if you think you need her."

"I'll look and text you. You just get moving. I'll meet you."

"I sort of hate this asshole." Every so often Matty said the most...asinine things.

"If you can, bring some food. Coffee. Thanks." He got the door for Jack and then gestured to Matt. They'd get moving first, and then once Matt was safe, he'd check-in with Matt a little more personally. "Come on. We'll need a ride."

"I'll follow your lead. I'm just trying to not have a repeat of this morning." Was it only this morning? Seriously?

"I could do without that myself. We'll just go radio silent until tomorrow." He arranged an unmarked car and they started driving. Jack's text came in quickly and said one word.

Rainbow.

Got it.

The apartment was clean but very small, and in a brownstone in Brooklyn. There was one bedroom and a pull-out couch, the shades were drawn and stayed that way. There was basic coffee in the cabinet, and Derek started a pot, letting them both just settle a little. Breathe. "Looks like we have powdered creamer but I'm going for black. You?"

"Black is fine." Matt stretched up, back popping and cracking.

"You know, if it weren't for this whole serial killer thing, I'd feel like a million bucks right now." He shot Matt a grin.

Matty glanced over at him, and he could see it, Matt fighting a smile. "Perv."

"Oh. Right. You tried to suck my soul out of my dick, but I'm the perv? Takes one to know one." He chuckled smugly and pulled a couple of mugs out of a cabinet.

"I like the way you fit on my tongue." The certainty found him clacking the mugs together.

Damn.

He set the mugs down extra carefully. "I like the way you just say what you're thinking. It's hot. Crazy, but hot."

"I'm not an exceptional liar. Can I kiss you?"

"Sure. I want to see how you fit on my tongue, too." He stepped over to Matt and ran his hands over that flat belly.

"Do you?" Matt rippled against his fingertips, almost like he was teasing his fingers, drawing them up toward the hard nipples.

"Uh-huh." Derek leaned close, plenty close enough for a kiss but didn't quite, lips hovering over Matt's, teasing. Matt's tongue flicked out, stroking his lips with a liquid heat.

He caught that tongue with his own and circled it, then slid them together until they caught each other in a kiss. Matt's hands slid around his waist, resting there on the small of his back, warm and heavy.

Derek closed his eyes and shut out everything, hanging there in the moment with Matt. Just the two of them and no rush, no worry. Nothing else. He held on to Matty's braid, letting the weight of his hand just give a little pull.

There was a knock at the door. Two taps, then three, then two more. Jack.

"Later." Derek broke the kiss off abruptly and headed back to the coffee maker as Jack keyed into the apartment.

"Hey. I've got the doctor's bag."

"Great. I was just making coffee, you want some?"

What he wouldn't give for a full, uninterrupted day with Matty. He wanted this goddamn nightmare over with.

"No. I want to go home and sleep, man. I have subs and chips, Cokes, cookies."

"Thanks. The cookies will make a great breakfast." He grinned at Jack and took the bags of food from him. "Go sleep. There are two guys on the block so we're good. My cell is off. Use the landline if you need me."

"On it. Keep your eyes open, boss. Try and rest."

He nodded. "Will do. Thanks for bringing Matt's bag. We'll see you at nine."

"Yep. Night." Jack stepped back out into the hall.

"Night." He closed the door and locked it with the deadbolt. "Okay. You can relax, now. We're safe here."

"Yeah? Good." Matt went to the sofa and sat, slowly working his braid loose.

He started unpacking the bags and putting things in the fridge. "You want some food? There's subs here and chips. Or just some coffee?"

"Coffee, right now. I'll have a sandwich in a bit."

Derek brought over two mugs and sat with Matt, admiring as all that hair fell around Matt's shoulders. He reached out and tangled his fingers in it. "Love this. Really."

"I love the way you touch it." There was no doubt that Matt had taken down his hair for Derek and no other reason.

Derek took a sip of his coffee and set the mug down, accepting the invitation to touch and combing his fingers through the dark length of Matt's hair. "So tell me something about Matthew Herrera that I don't know. Something not about work."

"When I was a little boy, my favorite thing on earth was to go to my 'uelita's and hunt ghosts with her."

"Is that your grandmother?" He guided the bulk of Matt's hair over one shoulder, loving the weight of it. "Did you find any?"

"We did. She helped them find their way out. That was her job." Matt rolled his head, his shoulders.

"Her job?" Cute. Kids were so gullible. "Did she tell you that? She must have been fun."

"I spent a lot of time with her, before I left for Houston. She was amazing."

He'd swear he felt Matt relaxing some. "Why did you move to Houston?"

"College. I did my doctorate work at Rice. My aunty let me stay with her as my guardian, you know? It didn't work out. I finished my thesis in rehab."

And Matt had met Ben in rehab. He knew where the rest of that story went. "And your parents are where, you said?"

"My parents are in Santa Fe, and they visit a lot." Matt chuckled softly, and the sound wasn't bitter at all, but warm, fond. "They're good people. Brilliant."

"Close is good? I have family not too far away too, but I like that they have to be selective about when they decide to visit." And his work was always a good excuse if he wasn't up for family.

"They call. It's a drive to just stop in."

"Ah. Good." He laughed and scritched his fingers across Matt's scalp. "What do they do that they are so brilliant?"

Matt leaned back toward him, moaning deep in his chest. "My father is an orthopedic surgeon, and mama is Dr. Benally, tenured sociology professor."

"Oh wow. They are brilliant. That's a tough act to follow, huh? Are they supportive?" He leaned forward and just breathed in the scent of shampoo and Matt, which was quickly becoming something important to him.

"You know, given that we have insane work schedules that never intersect, and I left home at twelve, they really are. They aren't concerned that I'm gay, they didn't kill me when I was a drunk, and they—" Matty stopped short, sighed softly. "They were willing to leave me alone after Ben because I needed that."

"Sounds like they love you." Derek pushed Matt's hair aside and kissed his neck. "I'm looking forward to going out there. I've never been."

"It's a special place. It hums, and the sky is beautiful." Matt's shoulders drew up and then relaxed. "That's all good, hmm?"

"All good." Derek slid his hands over Matt's arms. "What do you want more? Food, or rest?"

"I'm not hungry yet." That 'yet' gave Derek hope.

"Okay. Let's go put some sheets on the bed and close our eyes for a while then." Tomorrow was going to be a bad day. It didn't really matter what happened exactly, any way it played out was going to be stressful and draining and by tomorrow night they were all going to be well-fried. He hoped he could get Matty to really sleep, and some rest would be good for him too.

"Sounds good. I could just breathe for a little while. Let myself relax." Matty stood, held out one hand. "Come on."

He took the hand with a smile. That's exactly what they needed, to just breathe. Talk softly, take advantage of the temporary, but nonetheless real, safety. He followed along into the bedroom. It was tiny and dark, and Derek had to hunt a second for the lamp. The bed was only a double so they didn't have much option but to get friendly, and there was a stack of sheets and pillows and a folded blanket in the center of it.

But it was a bed. It would do fine.

They worked together easily. Hell, they managed to put the fitted sheet on without it springing back and popping anyone. That was damned miracle.

"Well. We made the bed, I guess we should lie in it." He laughed at himself because that joke was as stupid as it was ironic. Derek tugged his shirt off and lay it across the foot of the bed.

Matty didn't just chuckle; that laugh was a full-out belly laugh—surprised and out loud and tickled.

He gave Matty a triumphant smile. "Liked that one, huh?" He kicked his shoes off and rolled into bed, stretching out long. "Noted. Matty likes stupid puns."

"I do. The sillier the better. Don't tell my secret." Matt followed his lead, so tan and dark against the stark white pillowcase.

"Come here." He flopped an arm out over Matt's head. "We got hauled out of bed and didn't get to relax this morning. I'd like to just...hold you for a while if that's okay."

"Please. Has it been as long for you as it has for me?" Matt cuddled into him, deep breath relaxing him.

"For sex, no. Probably not. But this?" He tucked his arm around Matt's shoulders. "Maybe. Yeah. It's been a long while since I was with someone I wanted to wake up next to."

Waking up next to Matt was the least of it. He was making plans to visit New-Fucking-Mexico. Was he serious? What was this? A crush? An obsession? It felt so real but that seemed so ridiculous.

But Matt trusted him enough to sleep, to rest, and he didn't know whether anyone had given that to Matty in a decade. It felt good to be the guy that could.

"I think we have something here."

"I think you're right." Matt blinked up at him, dark eyes

meeting his. "I have all this shit to say and no way to say it. That doesn't happen often."

He nodded. "Yeah. I can't quite get a handle on it yet, or boil it down to words. I hear you." He thought they kind of knew, and the words would come eventually. "I've got you though, and it's absolutely safe here, I promise."

"I won't let him hurt you either. You have my word." Matt reached up, cupped his jaw.

"He's not going to hurt me." There might be threats to scare Matt, worry him. "Let's not bring him in bed with us."

"Good plan. There's not enough room." Matt kissed his jaw. "There's barely enough room for your shoulders and my head."

"Are you saying you have a big head?" He chuckled softly. "I hope your bed in New Mexico is bigger than this."

"It is. It's a king. My bedroom is my oasis. You're going to love it."

He could go right now. He really could. "Sounds like heaven." He kissed Matty's forehead. "Close your eyes. It would make me happy to see you sleep."

"Stay here, huh? Stay with me." That was a request he could handle.

"I will. I'm right where I want to be." He gave Matty's forehead another kiss and tangled his fingers in that luscious hair, listening as Matt's breathing evened out. He'd sleep too, once he was sure he wouldn't be the only one.

13

Matthew woke up with dread in the center of his forehead weighing him down. Something was wrong. He could feel it.

He sat up, looking out into the inky blackness of the room. He didn't see anyone, couldn't hear anyone breathing.

Wait.

He should hear Derek.

Matt closed his eyes, shutting out the darkness, letting himself focus on the flashes and streaks of light behind his eyelids while he tried to will himself to reach out and touch Derek, assure himself that he was still there.

All Matt had to do was reach out his hand and touch Derek.

But he couldn't.

What if he reached out, stroked his fingers down along Derek's belly and found the slick, wet ropes of intestines? What if it was like his Ben and he just found a pool of congealing blood soaking into the mattress, dripping through the coils in the box springs?

His stomach clenched, and he fought the tears that burned in his eyes.

A noise hit his ear—a gurgle, maybe?

You have to be brave. You have to move. You have to. If you sit here all night and panic, you'll die. You'll stroke out, and then you'll be found later, you and Derek rotting together in the dark.

Turn on a light. He tried to reach out, find the switch on the lamp.

A heavy arm curled over him and Derek nuzzled into his hair, his lover's heat moving close to his back. "Mmm. Got you."

"Oh God." He sucked in a deep breath, trying to calm his racing heart.

"Breathing is good. You were flailing around with your arm and muttering at me." Derek didn't move, even sounded still half-asleep. "Just a dream. I'm real."

Dreaming? He hadn't been dreaming, Had he?

"Mmhmm. Sorry." Jesus. He was losing his motherfucking mind. He was losing his mind, and there wasn't anything he could do about it.

"Don't be. Sleeping is good too." Derek laughed softly, so relaxed and easy, and not losing his mind at all.

Matthew nodded and settled, keeping his mouth shut. Sleep would be great, but he'd take sitting awake and watching without nightmares.

The room went quiet again and he lay there listening to Derek breathe. Neither of them even twitched until Derek suddenly took a deep breath. "What's the matter?"

"I just... I'm worried. I don't want either one of us hurt."

"Me neither." Derek tucked up tighter against him and spoke slowly and softly. "He's going to use me to try to get something from you. But he's not going to waste his energy on me. So, if he tries, you call his bluff. As for you, it's my job to keep you safe, and I am taking that very seriously. I'm sure it's no surprise that I'd like you in one piece too."

"No, you've made that clear. I appreciate that about you, in fact." This time his smile felt genuine. "It's a superior character trait."

Derek laughed, breath moving his hair. "Thanks. Your approval means a lot to me." The truth and the sarcasm in Derek's words lightened things up a little. "Okay, I'm awake now, you brat."

"Sorry. Our worlds are running on a weird mix of murder, sex, and adrenaline right now." And he wasn't sure what all the extra pieces were.

"I know. It's hard to stay grounded. I'm not sure what grounded even is right now. I'm going to say it's this."

If it was this—him and Derek—then it wasn't going to stay a secret for long. Everyone would know tomorrow. He wanted to know what it was that the bastard needed from him. He was ready to play the game and take Derek home with him.

"My sister's going to love you. She lives in Jersey and has the cutest little boy, my nephew Drew. Andrew. He's three. I think he's the first and only person in my life to like me on sight." Derek laughed. "She's a teacher, but she's really an artist. She does these huge mural things. Like, huge."

"Really? I would love to meet them." No one wanted to meet him. No one wanted him to meet their family. Ever. Not even Ben. Ben had a brother, but they'd never spoken.

"Maybe there will be some time before you go home. Drew is such a good kid. And Amy is...smart. Like you. And bookish. Introvert. Kind of a nerd." Derek found his hand and tangled their fingers. "Really. She'll like you."

"I haven't been anywhere in a long time. I'd like that. We

could go and see—you." He was an idiot. The smartest idiot he knew. He was going to fight with a serial killer tomorrow, and he was making plans to meet his lover's family.

Still, what was he fighting for if he didn't have something to look forward to?

"We could. And we could do some fun city stuff maybe. Statue of Liberty or Times Square. Lots of reasons for you to...uh." To what? Stay?

"If you'll come back with me. I want that. You. You should see my house."

"I want to see your house, see New Mexico. It sounds great. We're better off right now taking things day by day. Let's talk about...this, us...when we hit the back end of this thing." Derek tucked up tighter to his back, which said more than the words did.

"It's a plan." It was a ridiculous plan, and he knew it. This was stress fucking. Derek had a life and a career, and Matt had a gorgeous prison and enough money to live on with his periodic conference calls and his position in a think tank. Still, false hope was better than no hope at all. Hopefully tomorrow this shit would be over.

The phone on the nightstand rang, the sound shockingly loud in the quiet, dark room, and they both jumped.

"Jesus." Derek rolled over and answered it. "Wheeler." The room went quiet again for a long moment and, finally, Derek sighed. "We'll get moving. You come, Jack. I don't trust—right. See you soon."

Derek hung up the phone and turned on the lamp.

"What did he do?" He grabbed his jeans, his last clean shirt, telling himself that he'd known, hadn't he? Something was wrong. Someone was hurt.

"We don't know, but that phone he gave you has been

ringing off the hook for an hour. The precinct called Jack."
Derek was dressing too, right back into the clothes he'd
worn the day before.

"Did they get hold of him?" He tore the comb through
his hair.

"Yeah, he's on his way to get us." Derek peeked out the
side of the curtains and the bluish light of dawn filtered in.
"Well, we got a little sleep at least."

"I bet he's nice and pissed off now, huh?"

"Who, Jack?"

Matt shook his head. "Bald Adonai."

He figured the son of a bitch was screaming right about
now, and that was good. Angry people made mistakes.

"Good. He'll be off his game. It'll fuck with his plan,
whatever it is." Derek sighed, let the curtain go and gave his
hand a squeeze. "There's some toiletries in the bathroom,
I'm going to brush my teeth."

"I'll be here." Today was it. Today things were going to
change.

Derek closed the bathroom door and Matthew heard the
water running. A second later, the phone rang again.

He grabbed it without thinking. "Hello?"

"Matthew. You've been a bad boy. I've had to be quite...
firm with Detective Evers to get this address, haven't I, Jack?"

The scream was sharp and loud, turning his stomach,
and he looked to the bathroom. Nowhere was safe.

"What do you want?"

"You. I want you. Downstairs. Now. Or I cut off another
finger."

"Leave the officer alone. He's served his purpose." Matt
put the phone down carefully without severing the
connection and grabbed Derek's sidearm off the bedside
table.

Please stop me. Please walk out of the bathroom and say that I don't have to do this. Please.

But of course, Derek didn't. The door was closed.

He slipped out of the apartment and started down the stairs. Someone was going to die today.

Hopefully it wasn't him.

14

"Jack should be here any minute."

Derek stepped out of the bathroom. God, he was tired. But at least his teeth weren't fuzzy anymore.

"Matt?" Not in the bedroom. Probably making coffee. "Hey, listen. We can get coffee at the precinct. I don't think we have time for—"

Fuck. The front door wasn't closed. He stared at it. The fucking front door wasn't closed all the way.

Fuck.

He strode back into the bedroom for his gun and instead found it gone and the phone off the hook.

And now he had a choice. Pick up the receiver or just go after Matt. Goddammit! Why didn't he ever just know what to do? He decided more talk was a waste of his time and Matt couldn't have gotten far. He took off out the door and down the stairs, grateful that he still ran when he could.

He glanced around the lobby but didn't see anything and shouted for Matt as soon as he hit the sidewalk.

It took a heartbeat to understand what he saw, to parse out what his unbelieving eyes were telling him. There were three men in a standoff—Matt had Derek's sidearm drawn on a bald, shorter man in a hoodie. The bald guy was holding a bloodied beaten guy with pistol to his temple.

"Jesus Christ."

Okay this was bad. Like, people could die kind of bad and he wasn't going to help matters panicking about it. He took a deep breath and made himself think.

And that meant stall.

"What's going on here?" Derek looked between them. "Matt. Lower the gun."

"That would be a bad idea on my part. Jack here needs help." Matt's eyes never left the shorter man and the gun didn't waver.

"Jack?" That was Jack? *Oh, fuck.* "What do you want, asshole?"

"For starters? I know you have unmarked cars on this block, so I want to take this inside."

Shit. So much for that plan. His mind was going a mile a minute. He needed to get Jack out of this. The guy was unrecognizable and not too steady on his feet.

Oh.

"Listen. I'm worried about Jack. I've never seen him like that. He can barely stand up."

Derek glanced at Jack, hoping he'd heard, hoping he understood. Jack groaned, which was enough for him to know they were on the same page.

Matthew stepped toward Derek, and Baldy growled. "No moving."

"Fuck you, man." Matthew took another step, putting him within reach of his firearm.

"Don't move or I'll shoot him, I swear, Matthew." Baldy sounded a little desperate. Derek was pretty sure he'd gone rogue, this couldn't be been Adonai's plan. "Then his blood will be on your conscience too."

Derek eyed Matt's grip, then looked back at Jack. "It's okay, Jack. I've got this now."

Right on cue—*thank fuck*—Jack collapsed, going boneless and heavy in his captor's arms. Baldy lost his balance and was forced to lower the hand holding the gun to catch him. That was when Derek dove for his sidearm, dragging it from Matt's fingers, taking aim, and firing at the bald man's head.

Matty jumped for Jack as the guy fell, grabbing Jack and dragging him away.

"Be careful, Derek!" Matty shouted suddenly. Derek readied himself for another shot as the guy lifted his firearm but it never went off. The guy sank to his knees and fell over to one side, sprawling on the sidewalk. Both unmarked cars pulled up in an instant. Derek held his gun out to one side by the handle where it was easily seen, and his other hand up in the air.

"We're going to need two rigs." Derek pointed to Jack as one of the cops kicked the bald guy's weapon out of reach, then took his gun from him too.

"I'm going to lock this in my car, detective. I'll make the call."

The other cop he knew. "Sam. I understand protocol but I need to check on my man."

"Go ahead, sir. Rich and I both saw what happened."

Thank God for that. One less thing he was going to have to explain. Derek hurried to where Matt had Jack stretched out, head in his lap, and looked at Matt. "You okay?"

"Did you find his fingers?"

"Did—what?" *What?* His vision tunneled for a second. *Get it together, Crash. You don't get to lose it.*

He took a couple of uneasy steps toward the bald guy's body and reached for it. Fingers? Jesus Christ. This guy really was a sick fuck. And Jack didn't give anything up easy. Derek dug through the guy's pockets and actually came up with what he was looking for.

Don't puke. Do not puke.

Thankfully, he heard the ambulance siren, so he just stayed there and didn't move until someone came to him.

After that things got chaotic. There were questions and sirens, protocol and pictures, and he never did get to talk to Jack. Jack had been whisked away in an ambo and Matty— well, Matty he'd just lost track of. The sun was all the way up, watery behind the clouds, when he realized that Matt was nowhere to be found.

He tried Matt's cell before remembering they'd left it in the conference room and caught a ride to the precinct, struggling with the hollow feeling in the pit of his stomach. He needed to find Matt, touch him, look into his eyes. See for himself that Matt was okay.

When he got to the precinct, he had to ask four separate people but finally tracked Matt down, sitting alone in one of the holding rooms.

Matt was wearing a jumpsuit, paper shoes, his head was down, and a can of Coke was sitting in front of him. God, this had to be so hard, going through this shit again.

"Hey." Derek stepped through the door and let it close behind him. "I lost track of you, I'm sorry."

"Hey. They took my clothes for evidence. How's Jack?"

"I have a call in, but I don't know." He'd held Jack's fingers in his hand while standing ten feet away from the rest of the man. That was how Jack was. Bad.

"How are you?" He grabbed a chair and dragged it over,

metal feet scraping across the floor to sit next to Matt. "No bullshit. How are you really?"

Matt's eyes were on the ground. "I want my own clothes. I want a shower. I'm sorry people died because of me."

"A monster died, and I don't shoot innocent people, Matt." The bald guy, who still hadn't been identified as far as he knew, wasn't the first man he'd fired his gun at, but he was the first one Derek had killed. He was sorry it came to that, and not particularly proud of the fact, but he didn't feel terribly guilty for doing what he had to do either.

"I'm not talking about him. I'm talking about the others. I'm talking about Ben." Matt stared at him, dark eyes filled with tears.

He nodded, holding that gaze for a bit even though it was painful, even though he had no idea what to say. "Come home with me."

"Can I? Can we just go?"

How could he tell those devastated eyes no?

"Yeah. Yeah, we can go." He stood up, shoving his chair back with his knees. "We can go right now." He didn't care whether they really could or not. If someone needed Matt they could come back tomorrow. "Come on."

Matt stood, and it said something that his lover didn't even ask for his phone. He simply took Derek's hand and followed him.

Derek stopped by the conference room to grab it anyway and pulled Matt into a cab to head home. He had so many things to wrap up. Matt's bag was still at the safe house, he needed to talk to Jack and find out what had actually happened. He needed to find out how much of what happened was ordered by that asshole in prison.

Details could wait until tomorrow. Tonight was about Matt, it had to be. Nobody else was looking out for him.

And nobody else could do it like Derek could.

Matt sat in the cab, still and small, absolutely silent. Derek reached out, and Matt took his hand and held on.

At home Derek keyed in and ushered Matt straight to the bedroom where he pulled out towels. "You take your shower. Take as long as you need. I'm going to call the hospital and then put some soup or something on."

He wasn't hungry, but it was something to do. Maybe he'd have a beer. Or something stronger.

The water started and then he heard Matt get into the tub, and it didn't take a minute before the sobs started.

He stayed outside the bathroom door longer than he'd intended, listening, torn about whether he should knock or walk away. Sometimes a man wanted privacy, but sometimes he wanted comfort. He had no idea which one Matt needed more.

In the end he walked away, giving Matt time. And space. Letting Matt come to him.

His phone call to the hospital wasn't all that helpful. Jack was out cold, and no one would give him real information over the phone. He'd have to go by in the morning. He didn't make food; he didn't even have a beer. He ended up just standing in the kitchen, leaning against the sink, lost in his own thoughts.

Matt came in, wearing a towel, ashy and pale, hair down and mussed.

He looked up and caught Matt's eyes. For all his brooding in the last half an hour he hadn't come up with one goddamn thing to say that was going to help. Instead he held his arms open, offering the only thing he did have, himself.

Matt came right to him, pushing into his arms with a soft sound, face against his throat.

"I'm sorry." He sighed and held Matt close and tight. "But you can go home now. So can your parents, Mari... I can get you on a plane home as soon as tomorrow if you want."

"Can you come? If I stay a few days or no?"

Could he? Should he? He didn't want to let Matt go, that was about all he knew. He wanted to go. He wasn't sure he cared whether he should. "I'll need a little time to wrap things up here. I need to make sure Jack is okay. But then I can come. I think you should go, though. You don't belong here."

Matt looked up, met his eyes. "I'm sorry. I wish I'd been wrong."

"I hate to think how much worse this would have been if you weren't so insistent." He kissed Matt's forehead. "It's over now though. Maybe we can sleep in tomorrow."

"That would be something. Can I have a drink of water or a Coke or something?"

He took a deep breath. Whatever happened next was going to be theirs finally, and something kind of normal was a good place to start.

"Yeah. You want to borrow some clothes? I'll have your bag brought over in the morning." He let Matt go and got two Cokes from the fridge.

"Please, yes. Something warm?"

God. The last thing he wanted Matt to feel right now was cold. Derek realized suddenly that if he wanted all of this to feel less awkward, if he wanted them to be able to relax, it was on him. Matt was just out of reserves.

Instead of putting the drinks down, Derek walked to Matt, gave him a quick kiss and headed for the bedroom. "Come on, Einstein. Let's get you warmed up and find you that hairbrush."

"You—you're good to me. Thank you." The words were so soft, so gentle, almost nonexistent.

He let Matt follow him into the bedroom and set their drinks down so he could search up some sweats and a T-shirt. "These are on the small side for me, hopefully they'll work." He looked around for the hairbrush he'd lent Matt the other night.

"It's good to have a lover that's built like a brick house."

He liked the sound of 'lover' in Matt's round tones.

"I'm glad you think so." He kissed Matt again and handed off the clothes. "Lover. Sounds good when you say it, even if I am still trying to get my head around everything."

"You don't have to." Matt slipped his sweats on, wrapping himself up. "You didn't ask for me. Well, I suppose you did, in a very practical way…"

Except that he did have to. Or he had to try anyway. He was terrible at this; he didn't understand relationships, but he thought he understood Matt. He tangled one finger in a strand of Matt's hair. "Why are you saying that? Because you don't want me, or because you're worried I don't want you?"

Matt met his eyes, open and clear and direct as fuck. "I'm worried that we need each other. I'm worried that you woke me up, and when I go home I'm just going to go back to sleep again."

"I need you awake, so I guess it's my job to make sure that doesn't happen. I'm not worried about that. What worries me isn't the what or the why. It's the how." It was always the how with him, even with work. He often doubted his own ability to pull shit off. He wasn't sure why though, so far he'd done pretty well just winging it.

"That will figure itself out. At least it seems to. Maybe I just want it to. I don't have any way to know." Matt winked at him, and once more his lover lost years of pain and sorrow, all of a sudden.

"Can't profile this one, right?" Derek wanted it to work out too. That seemed like enough, at least for today. "The one thing we shouldn't do any more is worry. I don't know about you, but I've had enough of that. I'm looking forward to seeing New Mexico and your house. I'm looking forward to seeing how we play out, and to making my part happen. If you're in, I'm in, Matty."

"No one calls me Matty but you." Matt kissed him, the touch slow, painfully sweet. "I'm in, Officer."

The Cowboy and the Dom Series

Book One: First Rodeo

Book Two: Razor's Edge

Book Three: No Ghosts

If you enjoyed Cryptic, try First Rodeo!

FIRST RODEO, Book one

When a killer strikes, Texan and former rodeo cowboy, Sam O'Reilly, loses his older brother. Unbeknownst to Sam, James was also the lover and sub of a sophisticated New York City Dom named Thomas Ward. Sam comes to the city determined to stay until he can bring the murderer to his own brand of justice, while Thomas' more ordered mind is hoping for a legal solution. Neither man expects their connection to the other, but having each lost someone irreplaceable, their hearts are crying out for comfort almost as loudly as their bodies are screaming for each other.

Some yearnings refuse to be ignored, but transcending their differences to explore the fragile connection between them will prove to be a steep a hill to climb--the first of many. As Sam and Thomas take the first tentative steps on the rocky path that might lead to a relationship, the killer steps out of the shadows...And this time, his sights are set on Sam.

Note to our readers: Each of the three books in The Cowboy and the Dom Series has a fully realized, romantic ending. However, the overarching suspense element will leave readers on a cliffhanger after books one and two, to be fully resolved in book three.

RAZOR'S EDGE, Book 2

Razor blades left by a murderer continue to remind Sam and Thomas of James, the man they lost to violence... whose killer is still out there and seems to be watching them constantly, biding his time.

Meanwhile, their carefully built relationship also teeters on the edge of a knife. Sam's efforts to be the kind of full-time sub he thinks Thomas wants fail miserably, and Thomas must accept the fact that Sam is unique and his lover's needs don't lend themselves to the typical high protocol BDSM lifestyle. They contend with jealousy, confusion, arguments and stress, and when communication starts to break down, they struggle to reconcile their massive differences and learn what it means to be a them.

An emotional misunderstanding might be the last straw--or the opportunity the killer has been waiting for to take Sam out of Thomas's life once and for all.

Note to our readers: Each of the three books in The Cowboy and the Dom Series has a fully realized, romantic ending. However, the overarching suspense element will leave readers on a cliffhanger after books one and two, to be fully resolved in book three. Readers should begin the series with book one, First Rodeo.

NO GHOSTS, Book 3

Months after James's brutal murder, Sam gets an opportunity to help Thomas find closure. That means leaving New York City to travel to the O'Reilly's Texas home, to meet Sam's parents and get a taste of how and where the O'Reilly brothers grew up.

Their vacation is also an opportunity for Thomas and Sam to move beyond the past, drop their remaining baggage, and finally solidify their tumultuous relationship.

But that may be easier said than done given that Thomas has a secret he's been keeping from Sam, and Sam is sick and tired of everyone in his life knowing what's going on but him. It's the worst time for their trust to break down, because their final confrontation with James's killer looms, and if they're going to walk away, they'll have to do it together.

Note to our readers: Each of the three books in The Cowboy and the Dom Series has a fully realized, romantic ending. However, the overarching suspense element will leave readers on a cliffhanger after books one and two, to be fully resolved in book three. Readers should begin the series with book one, First Rodeo.

Interested in learning more about BA's cowboys and Jodi's gentlemen? Want free fiction and news? Join our newsletters!

What's Up with Jodi
http://bit.ly/whatsupjodi

Spurs and Shifters
https://lp.constantcontact.com/su/A9CRUzp/baandjulia

ABOUT JODI

JODI takes herself way too seriously and has been known to randomly break out in song. Her men are imperfect but genuine, stubborn but likable, often kinky, and frequently their own worst enemies. They are characters you can't help but fall in love with while they stumble along the path to their happily ever after. For those looking to get on her good side, Jodi's addictions include nonfat lattes, Malbec and tequila any way you pour it.

Website: jodipayne.net
Newsletter: http://bit.ly/whatsupjodi
All Jodi's Social Links: linktr.ee/jodipayne

ABOUT BA

Texan to the bone and an unrepentant Daddy's Girl, BA Tortuga spends her days with her basset hounds, getting tattooed, texting her grandbabies, and eating Mexican food. When she's not doing that, she's writing. She spends her days off watching rodeo, knitting and surfing Pinterest in the name of research. BA's personal saviors include her wife, Julia Talbot, her best friends, and coffee. Lots of coffee. Really good coffee.

Having written everything from fist-fighting rednecks to hard-core cowboys to werewolves, BA does her damnedest to tell the stories of her heart, which was raised in Northeast Texas, but has heard the call of the high desert and lives in the Sandias. With books ranging from hard-hitting GLBT romance, to fiery ménages, to the most traditional of love stories, BA refuses to be pigeon-holed by anyone but the voices in her head.

BA loves to talk to her readers and can be found at http://batortuga.com/ and her newsletter signup link is http://bit.ly/BAJulianews

AVAILABLE FROM JODI & BA

East Meets Westerns

(single titles)

Heart of a Redneck

Wrecked

Land of Enchantment

Window Dressing

Flying Blind

Special Delivery, A Wrecked Holiday Novel

Keeping Promises

The Cowboy and the Dom Trilogy

First Rodeo, Book One

Razor's Edge, Book Two

No Ghosts, Book Three

The Soldier and the Angel, a Cowboy and Dom Novel

The Triskelion Series

Breaking the Rules

Les's Bar Series

Just Dex

The Lone Star Series

Tending Tyler

The Collaborations Series

Refraction

Syncopation

Secrets and Whispers

Temptation Ranch

Puzzles Series

Cryptic, Book One